More praise for Sonia Levitin and
THE GOLEM AND
THE DRAGON GIRL

"Levitin's entertaining, well-written story . . . deals creatively with a number of significant themes."
—*Kirkus Reviews*

"The characters are engaging, and the book's pace is swift. . . . Levitin shows off her writing skill . . . [and] keeps readers entertained."
—*Booklist*

THE GOLEM AND THE DRAGON GIRL

Sonia Levitin

FAWCETT JUNIPER • NEW YORK

A Fawcett Juniper Book
Published by Ballantine Books
Copyright © 1993 by Sonia Levitin

All rights reserved under International and Pan-American Copyright Conventions. Published in the United States by Ballantine Books, a division of Random House, Inc., New York, and distributed in Canada by Random House of Canada Limited, Toronto.

Library of Congress Catalog Card Number: 92-27665

ISBN 0-449-70441-6

This edition published by arrangement with E. P. Dutton, a division of NAL Penguin, Inc.

Manufactured in the United States of America

First Ballantine Books Edition: September 1994

10 9 8 7 6 5 4 3 2

*With thanks to my friends
Marcianna K. Chang and Laureen B. Chang,
for their gracious help.*

1

*

Laurel and her parents sat in the living room with the real estate lady, Miss O'Malley. Laurel couldn't stand the woman. She was big and awkward. She smiled too much. When Laurel's parents spoke, Miss O'Malley leaned toward them with exaggerated interest, agreeing with everything they said.

"Oh, yes, Mrs. Wang, you're so right! I know what you mean, Mr. Wang; you're much better off with a substantial loan." They talked for hours, it seemed, without really getting to the point. The point was that Miss O'Malley had found buyers for their house, just as she had also found a new home for Laurel and her parents.

"Ah, I had a good feeling about this the moment I walked into your home, Mrs. Wang. It felt—" the woman scanned the air, as if to find the missing word hanging there—"lucky."

"Yes, it has been a lucky house for us," said Laurel's mother. "We would never sell, except that we need the extra space now. Of course, my parents must have their own rooms."

"Of course," said Miss O'Malley. "The Henderson house is perfect for you, with its in-law apartment. I

1

think you were very, very lucky to find it. And Laurel doesn't even have to change schools!"

Laurel didn't like the way Miss O'Malley drew her in, making her an accomplice to this dreadful thing she wanted no part of.

"Our daughter does not want to move," Laurel's father said gently, and he smiled at Laurel with his eyes only. Laurel felt her heart leaping in her chest. Why was her father opening up her pain for this strange woman to see? How could he! She wanted to run from the room. Instead, she shifted in her chair and made her face placid. To run away from a visitor would be shameful and rude. Later Laurel's mother would confront her, eyes snapping like firecrackers, hands on hips. "Tiger girl!" she would hiss. "So stubborn and wild! When are you going to learn self-control?"

So Laurel squeezed her hands together and took a very deep breath. She imagined herself sitting in the orchestra pit, playing with the Youth Symphony. The notes from her flute would cascade over all the other players, drawing everyone together. Sometimes when she was angry, like now, Laurel let the music from her flute bounce up against the ceiling, until her strong feelings exploded into a thousand harmless little pieces, like confetti.

"It will be an adjustment, of course," Miss O'Malley said, "for Laurel to have her grandparents here. I must say, I think it's a wonderful heritage you have, this deep respect for the elderly."

"If a family has an old person in it," quoted Laurel's mother, "it possesses a jewel."

Laurel scowled. All her life she had heard such

words. But they were only words. Laurel had never known an old person. Her father's parents were dead, and her mother's parents had never left China. Yet she was expected to love and revere them and to accept them into her home.

Her mother continued soberly, "My parents have waited ten years to come here."

"Ten years!" exclaimed Miss O'Malley, her blue eyes shining with pretended interest. "Why so long?"

"The United States has a quota on Chinese immigrants," said Laurel's father, but he said it without reproach. It was only by his smile that Laurel could see his distress; Miss O'Malley got the opposite impression, of course.

"You have all been very patient," said the real estate lady. She gathered some papers together, ready for business.

Laurel's mother nodded. "Now, what about these people? Do you think we should consider their offer?"

"You could possibly counter, bring them up a few thousand dollars more," said Miss O'Malley. "The man is an insurance salesman. They have been married only a short time—the woman was widowed many years ago. She works for a recording company in San Francisco. Her son is twelve or thirteen, just starting junior high school."

"Just like our Laurel!" Laurel's father said warmly. "They sound like nice people."

"They love your house," said Miss O'Malley. "Absolutely love it—the trees, the yard, the porch. They'd like to come back on Sunday and bring their son to see it too. What do you think?"

"Tell them we want six thousand more," said Laurel's mother. She stood up, indicating that she would bargain no further. She was the business head of the family. As a banker she knew when to bargain or to close a deal, and it was always clear to Laurel when she had made a decision, because she stood up, raising herself to her full height. She was only five foot two inches; Laurel was already an inch taller than her mother. But size had nothing to do with power, as Laurel well knew.

Laurel's father stood too, backing up his wife.

"Very well," said Miss O'Malley. "I will tell them."

"Six thousand more," said Laurel's mother distinctly. "And we need to have their answer by the end of the week, so we can follow with our offer on the Henderson house."

"Of course," said the realtor.

Laurel and her parents accompanied the woman to the door and stood properly waving as she got into her car and drove off.

Laurel's mother turned to her, pointing. "Twenty minutes," she said. "Chinese school. Put on a skirt."

"Do I have to go?"

"Don't start that again, Laurel," her mother snapped. "Of course you have to go."

"The kids laugh at me. They're rude. Whenever I make a mistake . . ."

"Then don't make mistakes, Laurel," said her mother, "and nobody will laugh."

Jonathan hopped onto his bike and sped along the streets of Westvale, the tract where he had lived for as long as he could remember. "Fortunately, we had the house," Jonathan's mother always said. It made things

4

just a little easier after his father had died when Jonathan was only three.

The little house was cramped now, with Steve and his exuberance and all that equipment. Steve had moved in with a stationary bike, a punching bag, and a rowing machine.

Westvale houses were tiny cracker boxes, each one alike, so that the local joke had it a man could enter the wrong house, eat at the wrong table, sleep in the wrong bedroom with the wrong wife, and leave in the morning, never knowing the difference. The houses were so close together that you could hear the neighbors sneeze. But of course there were compensations. Here Jonathan had plenty of friends. Here he played with a great baseball team. Best of all, Uncle Jake lived within biking distance away in the flat little town called Colma.

Now Jonathan let the downhill grade take him. He loved to feel the wind against his face. He loved the bike ride to his uncle's place—some surprise always awaited him there.

But it was the beginning of the end. Jonathan felt it in his bones; this time the deal for the house was going through.

For the past six months, ever since his mom and Steve had gotten married, they had looked for a new home. Sometimes Jonathan went along, always annoyed when the realtors assumed that Steve was his dad.

How could anybody make such a mistake? All his life Jonathan had imagined what a father would be like. In Jonathan's mind the ideal father was a mixture of various men he had seen in movies: a young judge

5

who found humorous and wise solutions to people's problems; a baseball player who overcame his poor beginnings to become one of the greats; and his favorite, born of the gods into a crystal landscape, Superman.

Steve was a total nerd. When he wasn't fussing and fixing everything in sight—constantly screwing in light bulbs and adjusting doorframes—he cooked awful things, like carrot juice and sunflower burgers. Once he scooped out a pumpkin in which he cooked a horrible orange soup with dark lumps floating in it, like huge cockroaches. Of course, Jonathan refused to eat it.

Steve was even after Uncle Jake. "Listen, buddy," he said, "you'd better get some of that gut off, before you have a heart attack. If you're not gonna take care of your body, at least let me sell you some insurance!"

From day one Jonathan couldn't figure out what his mother saw in Steve. But she must have seen something, because they'd known each other for only about two months before they were off to Palm Springs for a long weekend honeymoon, during which Jonathan stayed with his uncle Jake.

Jonathan had tried to reason with his mom. "Why do you have to get married?"

She answered his question with a question. "Won't it be nice to have a man around the house?"

"We don't need a man. We have Uncle Jake."

"Uncle Jake doesn't live with us."

"I'm sure he would. Why don't we ask him?"

"Are you kidding?" His mom pushed back her dark hair and made a face. "I'd rather move to Siberia."

"That's horrible!" Jonathan yelled. "He's your own brother!"

"So, he's my brother," Mom said. "But we don't always see eye to eye. He's fire and I'm water. He's the fox and I'm the hen—don't you see? It would never work out."

When the talk of moving began, Uncle Jake only waved it aside. "Don't worry, Jonathan. Things always have a way of working out."

"How can it work out?" Jonathan cried. "I don't want to move. I've got friends here. I've got you. Why can't I stay here and live with you, Jake?"

"Tut-tut-tut, don't carry on, Jonathan. You know that would break your mother's heart. She loves you. She'll work things out for you, don't worry."

Uncle Jake never worried. That was one of the things that drove Jonathan's mom crazy. "He's like a child, for God's sake!" she'd rave. "His place is a shambles. And when did he last do a decent day's work?"

Work? Jonathan was amazed at how much Uncle Jake got done. He was always building something, or composing a new song, or poring through music books in the library. He revived old tunes from Eastern Europe and taught them to the musicians in his band.

"Klezmer," Uncle Jake said, delighted over his latest passion. "The music of a people. Soul. Jewish soul."

Uncle Jake and his band played for weddings and bar mitzvahs and gatherings of old folks. Oh, how those people nodded and tapped their feet, loving the music from their past! Sometimes Jake took him

7

along, and Jonathan would stand on the sidelines, clapping his hands and watching all those old people nodding over their memories. He himself had never known any old people. His dad's parents lived in Canada. His mom's parents were long dead. "I bring those people their youth," said Jake, "in a song. I love to make them happy!"

Jonathan's mom obviously didn't appreciate her brother. "Jake is a regular couch potato!" she complained. "If he doesn't go on a diet, he'll be sorry."

Jonathan let his bike flop down on the skimpy, small patch of grass in front of Jake's place. From inside came a strange noise, a vibration, a disjointed squeak.

Jonathan pushed the door open, heard the swirling, wildly ranging tones of a new instrument. It looked like a squashed potato. Jake stood in the middle of the room, his full face puffed and perspiring, hair curled against his collar, unruly and damp from the effort of blasting out this melody.

In the background came the accompaniment of the klezmer band, on cassette tape, loud and rousing. Instantly Jonathan wanted to dance.

"Hey!" Jonathan yelled. He strode into the room, which was choked with newspapers, books, pamphlets and catalogs, stamp albums, and all sorts of stuff and junk that seemed to multiply under Jake's touch.

Uncle Jake gave Jonathan a nod, never missing a beat.

"What's that?" Jonathan yelled above the music.

"Ocarina!" yelled Uncle Jake. He gestured with his eyes toward the pile of percussion instruments. Jake

8

stamped his feet as he played, making his stomach jiggle.

Jonathan was without musical ability when it came to horns, strings, or keyboards. But he could certainly beat the heck out of a drum or a tambourine, and this he did, echoing Uncle Jake's joy until the two of them were clearly celebrating New Year's Eve, though it was only September.

They met the beat of the klezmer band. They stamped and twirled and cried out, "Hey! Hey! Hoo-hoo!"

They leapt onto the kitchen chairs, then jumped down again. They pulled the cushions from the sofa and imagined them into plump women, dancing round and round and round. With a sudden groan Jake fell to the floor in a heap, gasping and pop-eyed.

Jonathan ran to him, scared to death.

"Uncle! Uncle!" Jonathan ran to the telephone. "I'll call 911!"

"No! No," wheezed his uncle, pulling himself up. He coughed and spat into a handkerchief. He pointed to the bathroom. "Just get my—inhaler."

A few minutes later Uncle Jake was settled back into his usual chaos, shuffling through papers, looking for his cigars.

"Should people who have asthma smoke cigars?" Jonathan asked, annoyed.

"You're beginning to sound just like your mom," said Jake.

"She tells me I'm starting to sound like you," Jonathan retorted. He held his breath against the dense cloud of cigar smoke. He coughed.

"So, pretty soon you won't have to be bothered by

my cigars," Jake said. "Your mom tells me they found a house. A beautiful place in Mill Valley. Trees. Playing fields. You're getting a dog."

"Big deal," Jonathan said. "I know what they're doing. The dog is a peace offering. To soften me up. Jake . . ." Jonathan paused. He looked down at the battered rug. "Couldn't I live with you?"

"Hey, buddy! We've been through all that."

"If I can't live with you, then come with us," Jonathan said. "Why won't you? You could get yourself an apartment in Sausalito. Then I could still take my bike and come to see you."

"I can't live in Sausalito. Rents are sky-high. And besides, what about my friends? The musicians? My chess partners? And the junkyard down in south San Francisco where I get my parts?"

"I need you," Jonathan said. He sighed, let out a groan, swayed to and fro. "How can I study if you're not there?"

"You'll study with the rabbi, like all the kids."

"You know I'm not going to do that," Jonathan said. "I want to learn with you. Like I've been doing. I'm way ahead of those kids. You said so yourself."

Jake pulled himself up to the sofa. "Look, Jonathan," he said, wiping his forehead with a large handkerchief, "don't make bargains. You do what you have to do. You'll enroll in a regular Hebrew class over there in Marin County, and when you have your bar mitzvah . . ."

"I won't," said Jonathan. "My mom doesn't even care, and you can't force me."

"I can ask you," said Jake, momentarily closing his eyes. "I am asking you. Please."

10

"No. I went to Hebrew school once. It was awful. Chaos. The kids act like wild apes. Throwing things. I won't go!" Suddenly Jonathan found himself crying.

Flustered, Uncle Jake patted his pockets, nearly sat on his cigar, frowned, rubbed his hair until it stood on end. "Now, now, don't go and do that," he fussed. "You know how I hate that. What's wrong, buddy?"

Then Jonathan let it out, the thing that had stuck in his chest like a thorn all day, all week. "Steve wants to adopt me," he said. "He wants me to change my name to his. Be my *father*! I don't want him for a father. Can't he get that?"

Jake lay back against the soft sofa cushions. He shook his head. "Take it easy on him," Jake said. "Your mom loves him."

"Ha! Just like she loved all those other nerds."

"She is married to him. This is different."

"Not if I can help it," muttered Jonathan.

"So, what are you going to do?" Jake eyed him suspiciously. "You're going to sabotage this marriage? Look, Jonathan, you're putting me in a terrible position. Give it a good try, Jonathan. Your mom is going all the way for you, even agreeing to a dog."

Jonathan fumed. "She's even telling me what kind of dog to get. Steve wants a Dalmatian."

"So, nobody said you can't pick your own dog. Listen, I'll take you shopping for a dog. Here. Shake on it."

They shook.

"You'd better go," Jake said. "I've got a gig tonight."

"Are you going to be okay?"

11

"Sure. Nothing wrong with me that a good laugh won't cure!"

Jonathan smiled, but it was a phony smile. What if Jake had an asthma attack, who would be around to help him? Who would come biking straight down the hill in ten minutes flat? Nobody, that's who.

2

✳

"They want another six thousand dollars," said Jonathan's mother. She stood at the stove, wearing black jeans and a purple T-shirt with a logo that said NO SWEAT on it. "What are we going to do?"

"We offered them three thousand more," said Steve. He gave Jonathan a wink.

His mom turned to them, brought a platter of fried tofu to the table. "What's this?" asked Jonathan.

"Jonathan, don't start," said his mother. "Take some pickles and mustard. Help yourself to a bun. It'll taste just like a hamburger."

"Then why don't we just have hamburgers?" grumbled Jonathan. "Jake was having hot dogs."

"He's courting an early death," said Mom.

"At least he enjoys living," said Jonathan.

"Don't talk with your mouth full," said his mother, slathering her tofu patty with mustard and sprinkling sunflower seeds on top of it. "What if they don't go for it?" she asked her husband. "Three thousand more is our absolute limit."

"Don't worry," said Steve. "They need to sell." He helped himself to a burger, stuffed it between the two sides of a bun, and took a big bite. "Delicious, my darling," he said to his wife with a wink.

13

Jonathan gagged. He hated those winks.

"The way I see it," said Steve, "they asked for six thousand because they hope to get three. If there's one thing I know, it's business."

Jonathan hated that phrase too: "If there's one thing I know . . ." Steve was always saying it.

"I want that house," said Mom. "I love that house. Plenty of space. Jonathan can have his dog."

"Uncle Jake had another 'episode' today," Jonathan said, and he watched his mother's reaction.

She froze, and her eyes widened. Then, coolly, she asked, "Well, what was he doing? Swinging from the chandelier?"

"We were just playing some music," Jonathan said. "He collapsed. I had to get his inhaler for him. It's a good thing I was there."

"He should get some real exercise," said Steve. "And quit smoking. I tell you, the man's twenty-five pounds overweight, and he refuses to buy insurance."

"He doesn't want your insurance," Jonathan muttered. "He's sick, and all you guys do is pick on him."

"So he had another asthma attack," said Jonathan's mom. "He brings these on himself! What'd he do afterward? Smoke a cigar?"

Jonathan clamped his mouth shut. How did she always know?

"You don't have to answer, I smelled it on your clothes the minute you walked in. Listen, that brother of mine is impossible. He never grew up."

"That's why he shouldn't live alone," Jonathan said.

"The kid's got a point," said Steve.

"You!" Jonathan's mom pointed a long, red-tipped

14

finger at her new husband. "Don't you start in on me! I couldn't live with Jake for a single day."

"Jake should find himself a wife," said Steve. "Get a place of his own and settle down."

"You know I've tried to fix him up with a dozen women," said Jonathan's mother. "It's always a disaster. That crazy music of his. Those pals, those clothes!"

"Talk about crazy clothes," Jonathan said. "Look at you." His mom used to wear a soft blouse with a lacy collar, and a long skirt that swished when she walked. That was so long ago that Jonathan wasn't sure he hadn't dreamed it.

"Young man, that's enough!"

The phone rang. Jonathan's mother grabbed it once. She listened. Her face broke into a grin. "Really? Really? Terrific!"

She ran up to Steve, put her arms around him. "Darling, they accepted. The house is ours! Oh, Steve!" And they started to kiss.

Jonathan turned away, disgusted.

"Hey, Jonathan," called Steve, his arm still around Mom. "Let's you and me go shopping for that dog this weekend."

"No, thanks," said Jonathan. "I've already got a dog picked out."

He felt the tension, heard a sigh.

Jonathan went to his room. On his desk lay all the assembly parts for his new model, Mogul the Muscle Man. Along the wall at the back edge of the table stood his completed models, several classic cars, complete with real windows and decals, some planes, and his favorites: Superman, Scorpio the Skeleton Man,

15

and Ivan the Inner Man, a completed see-through figure with all the body organs visible under a pink transparent skin.

He sat staring at the picture of Mogul the Muscle Man, wondering how it would feel to have all that power. He certainly knew what he'd do with it—pulverize Steve.

The only good thing about Chinese school was driving across the Golden Gate Bridge, which Laurel and her mother did every Saturday. While Laurel was imprisoned in that small upstairs schoolroom with ten other kids and the kindly but weak-voiced Mrs. Chen, Laurel's mother went to Union Square, shopping for cosmetics or clothes, getting her hair trimmed, doing all the things she never had time for during the week.

"You never have time for me, either," Laurel wanted to say. But she knew better than to complain. Besides, her mom thought the twenty-five-minute drive from Mill Valley to Chinatown was "quality time."

Laurel's mother was very precise; time to her was a series of little boxes to be filled and then evaluated. To Laurel time was a succession of hound dogs closing in on her, yelping and crowding her into a corner.

Between chores and flute lessons, Chinese school and her regular homework, there was hardly any time unstructured. "Children need structure," Laurel's mother often said.

"They also need time for friends," her father objected once.

A deep color came to her mother's cheeks; she did not take well to being contradicted. "Better to have

16

one real friend," she snapped, "than twenty mere acquaintances."

They drove up the Waldo Grade. "You did not like Miss O'Malley," Laurel's mother said.

Laurel gazed out over the hills, now brown and golden. The autumn rains hadn't yet begun. The bridge, with its orange towers, rose just ahead of them.

"It showed in your face. You must learn better self-control, Laurel. Miss O'Malley was a guest in our home, after all."

"Yes, Mother," said Laurel.

Laurel caught her mother's glance. It was filled with sudden concern. "I know you don't want to move," she said. "Are you upset about leaving your friends?"

"What friends?" Laurel said bitterly.

"Isn't Polly your friend? You two have known each other since second grade. And what about Rita and Rachel? They are your friends, aren't they? You can invite them over when we move."

"Oh, sure. As long as we don't make any noise."

"Laurel. You are being difficult."

"Well, it's true," Laurel said. "I always have to be quiet. And when your parents come . . ." The little time she had with her mother would evaporate. The old people would demand her mother's attention. They would be annoyed by the sounds of Laurel and her friends talking and playing. Her home would become a prison.

"Now, Laurel, you are not being fair. You are a very lucky girl," her mother said. They drove onto the bridge, merging into traffic. "Your grandmother is a beautiful and wise woman. You will learn a great deal from her. And your grandfather also knows hundreds of wonderful stories. I have felt very poor without them," she said softly. "I wanted them to know you, Laurel, and you to know them. Now all my prayers . . ."

A sharp horn intruded, and Laurel's mother spun the car into the tollbooth lane, leaving her phrase unfinished.

The car sped along the bridge, past the Presidio with its tall pines and sparse military buildings. Laurel's mother drove down Broadway, past the many restaurants and cafés and bookstores and people all rushing about, doing errands.

The car slipped past the Chinese apartment buildings with their pagodalike roofs painted red, green, and bright yellow. Laurel's heart leapt in spite of herself at the beauty, the pleasant humor. Each Saturday she was pulled into this ancient world with its steep sidewalks and shops and open-air stalls. Sometimes Mother took time to let Laurel browse through the shops, especially when Mrs. Chen gave Laurel a compliment in her high, bell-like little voice.

In the shops Laurel felt truly transported, fingering the carved jade ornaments and lacquered boxes, the gilded figurines and beautiful porcelain rice bowls. She loved the smell of fresh white bean cakes and the salty dried fish. But that was only one part of her. The other part, the part that was four generations American, on her father's side, was embarrassed by the tottering old Chinese women who walked behind their husbands on tiny slippered feet. Or the men with their long mustaches hanging down to their chests, shaking

18

their fists at the chaos of children dodging between cars. They looked different, these people, creased and delicate, as if they had been pressed between the pages of huge old books. One came hobbling by now, wearing a padded vest and an ancient-style cap.

Laurel's cheeks burned. She felt embarrassed.

Suddenly she had a thought. "Mother, why can't Grandmother and Grandfather live here in Chinatown? Surely they'd be happier here, with other Chinese people."

"Laurel! What a terrible thing to say!" Her mother leaned toward Laurel, eyes flashing. "You think I would so dishonor my parents as to cast them out of my own home? For shame! How can you be so selfish? Sometimes I don't understand how it is that you are my daughter. They would take you in anytime. Like my auntie took me—do you feel nothing of the family tie?"

"But they won't like it!" Laurel burst out. "They won't like me!"

Her mother drew back, shaking her head. Then she took a deep, resolute breath. "Of course they will. How can you think that of *my parents*? They will love you, Laurel. Try, just try to withhold judgment. You haven't even seen them."

"I'm sorry, Mother," Laurel said humbly. "Truly I am."

But deep inside she wasn't sorry. She was only worried that her mother might not stop today for fortune cookies. And Laurel needed a fortune, desperately.

That night something awakened Laurel. Good, she thought. She got up, reached into the bag of fortune

19

cookies on her desk, and took one out. With it she crept softly down the hallway to her father's study.

Years ago, when they first bought this house, Laurel's father had installed the window seat here and covered it with a bright red cushion.

Father had told her, "This is your place, Laurel. Whenever you want to, you may come in. We will be together without speaking in this room." It was his study, where he worked on his architectural plans.

Laurel often came here at night, or on Saturday mornings when her father was out playing golf. Then she brought her flute and sat in the window seat playing softly to let the notes waft out the window and encircle the great oak tree that was Great-grandfather's home.

Now Laurel sat down on the window seat and gazed out at the moon. It hung in the sky like a silver platter, companion to the brass mirror on the opposite wall where her father's desk stood.

Laurel heard the wind chimes through the half-open window. She saw the slim shafts twirling in the breeze, and she heard the twinkling sounds almost as if they were coming from within the tree itself.

"Great-grandfather," Laurel whispered. She narrowed her eyes, so that the moon, the chimes, and the oak branches merged.

"Great-grandfather!" she said half aloud. "I need you. They sold the house. I don't want to leave you! What shall I do? Maybe you'll come with us to the new house. Will you? Will you?"

The moon floated high over the rooftops, sending its gentle light between the leaves and branches of the oak.

Now Laurel drew the Chinese character Peng, for peace, on the windowpane. Great-grandfather's name, Lin Peng, meant "peace in the forest."

He had sent a gift for Laurel before he died, knowing that his great-grandchild was on the way. The gift was a pair of golden dragons. Their bodies bent toward each other, but their heads turned outward to guard the home.

Ever since she could remember, the twin dragons had stood on the mantle, underneath Great-grandfather's portrait. His face, those gentle eyes and firm brows, were so real to Laurel that it seemed impossible that she had never known her Great-grandfather while he was still alive.

One thing was certain: He had loved her. He had prepared her gift the moment he knew she was expected on this earth. The gift was very precious and most significant. The dragons were intended to protect her, to guard her against evil.

Laurel held her breath, counting slowly to nine, the magic number. Slowly she exhaled, broke open the fortune cookie, and read the message.

"A lean dog shames his master," said the fortune.

What? What kind of a fortune is that?

The chimes tinkled like laughter. "Patience," came a whispering sound. "Contemplation—you will learn. Look for the deeper meaning. Don't be satisfied with surface thoughts. Be wise!"

The door sprang open. Light blazed into the room.

"What on earth are you doing?" Laurel's mother scolded. "How do you expect to get up in the morning and pay attention in school when you don't sleep at night?"

Mother's eyes lit on the fortune, the white curl of paper sharply exposed against the red cushion. She snatched it up. "What's this? Eating cookies? Here? Now?"

With her long, red fingernails Laurel's mother uncurled the fortune and, squinting, she read: "A lean dog shames his master."

She stared up at Laurel. Then she burst out laughing. "Well, you needn't worry about that, darling." She went to Laurel, drew her near, and led her gently from the room. "You'll never have any dog, fat or lean; why, dogs have terrified you since you were a baby."

At the doorway Laurel's mother snapped out the light. From the tree Laurel heard the tinkling sound of laughter. Cast against the wall she saw a silvery shadow that hovered for a moment in the moonlight, then swiftly disappeared.

3

*

It all happened so fast! A few handshakes, tea and sesame cookies, light laughter, and suddenly Laurel's house belonged to someone else, to this odd family with the hippie mother in her black jeans and ponytail, the serious father with the small wire glasses, and that boy, Jonathan.

They came over on Sunday. Jonathan kept exclaiming, "Wow!" and, "Gee whiz," and stomping through the house as if it already belonged to him.

The adults were so pleasant to one another, they might have been acquainted for years. Laurel's parents kept offering to let Jonathan's parents come over to inspect the plumbing, the roof, the cellar—and Jonathan's parents kept giving each other those mushy looks, saying how happy they were with the house. It made Laurel sick.

Once when they were carrying on that way, Laurel and Jonathan exchanged a quick glance followed by a mutual grin.

Maybe, Laurel thought, the boy wasn't so bad.

Two days before moving day Laurel had to get her things packed. Her mom was at work; good thing, she could never tolerate this commotion. Her father's friends from the neighborhood filled the house and yard, bringing cartons and paper and tape, laughing and giving advice.

Laurel's father had already taken most of her things to the new house. Her new room was freshly painted a pale blue. Her mom had bought lovely floral curtains and a matching bedspread. It was beautiful, Laurel had to admit it. Into the built-in glass cabinet Laurel put her collection of stone animals and her three trophies, one for spelling, two for music.

"Your grandparents will be so proud of you," her mom remarked, looking over the trophies. "Your teacher, Miss Windemann, thinks you have a good chance of being accepted into the Youth Symphony—if you keep on practicing, Laurel. Won't that be an honor?"

Laurel only nodded. Didn't her mother realize that she didn't need to be reminded? She had spent the past two years attending every performance of the Youth Symphony that she could. She watched the young musicians with an eager, critical ear and eye, and worked with her teacher on the same passages over and over.

"I think you can handle it, Laurel," Miss Windemann said. "If you make it, you will be one of the youngest musicians in the entire orchestra."

Tryouts were just two weeks away. Miss Windemann had increased her lessons to three a week, in preparation. At least, Laurel thought, I'm not nervous. She had discovered her own way of dealing with performances.

"I love to watch you play, Laurel," her mom used to say. "You look completely entranced. I suppose that is why you are never nervous or afraid."

How tender her mother could be at times! It was

only lately, since that letter had come from China, that the tension made her mother so sharp. Why, if she was so happy about her parents coming here, was her mother so cross lately? So unreasonable?

Now Laurel packed her special possessions—her new notebooks and pens, all ready for the first day of school; her new backpack; her small satin embroidered jewelry box containing her favorite hair ornaments and her jade necklace.

Laurel remembered the day, about a year ago, that she and her mother bought the beautiful jewelry box at the little gift shop in the Japanese Tea Garden. The Tea Garden was their favorite place. They used to go there often to stroll among the ferns and miniature trees, up over the wooden bridge that crossed a small stream where spotted golden carp darted between the reeds in the water. They would go up the narrow path to the pagoda, where cookies and jasmine tea were served by Japanese women wearing kimonos. Sometimes they would sit for a whole hour talking and watching the people go by.

That particular day her mother had talked about Auntie Meg, who had taken her in as a small girl. "Auntie was always busy, running the bed-and-breakfast inn, you know," Laurel's mother had said, her eyes distant with remembering. "But sometimes she took me out for tea or shopping, and then she always bought me a little treasure, something to save and remember her by. So," her mom had said gaily, "let's go get ourselves something special to remember this day!" And Laurel chose the red satin embroidered box, and her mom chose a deep blue scarf with a peacock on it.

Now Laurel held the jewelry box in her hand, and her throat tightened. Why do the good times always pass? she thought. She opened the jewelry box, took out her jade necklace, and fastened it around her neck. It made her feel better. Also, she didn't want to risk losing it during the move. She needed all the protection she could get, and jade was a well-known lucky charm. Of course, Laurel would carry her flute with her. It was the one thing Laurel would never entrust to anyone.

Suddenly she remembered the wind chimes and raced into her father's study, which, empty of its books and papers and ornaments, looked ugly and cold.

On the wall where the Chinese brass mirror had hung was a round pale spot. She remembered when her father first hung the mirror there, at the advice of Mr. Wu, the fêng shui man. It was many years ago, when they had first bought this house, and Laurel's mother called him to check out the placement of things, for Mr. Wu was a professional adviser.

"You must move your desk, Mr. Wang," the fêng shui scholar had said, "so that it does not face the door. Put it catercorner, so," and Mr. Wu had demonstrated, using arms, body, and legs. "I don't like that white wall. White is the color of death, you know. I advise you change it to a light beige, unless you want your business here to perish."

The fêng shui man had loved the window seat. "The red cushion! Very good, very good," he said, rubbing his hands together. "But a mirror on the back wall—that is a must. Otherwise, when the child sits in the window seat her body would be directly in line

26

with the sharp angle from this alcove. A brass mirror is definitely called for."

"What's all this going to cost us?" Laurel's father had asked, joking.

Laurel had seen the sudden fire in her mother's eyes, and she remembered Mr. Wu's swift response. "Merely a token," said he, "compared to the good health of your precious daughter."

So they had all gone to Chinatown and bought a beautifully designed brass platter for the wall. At the same time Laurel's mom had picked out the wind chimes and hung them in the oak tree.

Now Laurel stood upon the window seat and opened the window. From below she heard her father's voice and the shouts of the packers, but she could see only the thick limbs of the oak tree and the small grassy slope of the side yard and the fence.

"Great-grandfather," she whispered. "It's me. I'm going to take the wind chimes. Follow them. You like the sound. I know you do."

Laurel reached out, and as she lifted the chimes gently from the branch, she heard a sudden harsh crack, and she watched the branch fall down below onto the grass. The chimes remained in her hand.

A strange premonition told her she must leave the chimes here.

Trembling, Laurel replaced the chimes on a higher branch.

A thought came to her. Music. Music to soothe the savage beast—why not to entice the spirit out of the tree? She would play a beautiful melody, then take the wind chimes, place them inside her treasure box— with them, then, might come the spirit. Why not?

The ghost had come all the way from China, some-how, perhaps in the box along with the golden drag-ons. Why wouldn't it move again, wishing to be with its loved ones?

Laurel ran from the room and went to get her flute.

Going past the kitchen, she took a fortune cookie out of the bowl and slipped it into her pocket.

Upstairs Laurel stood for a moment, simply breath-ing, thinking the sweetness and the effortless sliding, floating, lifting of notes. Sometimes she could see them, almost, hanging in the air. Then she whispered a scale into her instrument, and heard the silvery notes emerge.

As Laurel played, the commotion from outside re-ceded and disappeared. She played and played, imag-ining another time, another country, another home. She imagined the Great-grandfather in the portrait, his wide brow and deep, knowing eyes, the serene mouth and firm features. She was lost in song, at one with the spirits and her own nature.

A sudden noise made Laurel turn. Startled, she stopped short, so that the notes seemed to come crash-ing to the floor. "What?" she gasped aloud. "What are you doing here?"

It was Jonathan.

"I'm sorry if I'm butting in," he said. "My mom and I came to measure the rooms. Your dad said to go right in. Say, you're really good. I've never heard any-body play the flute like that. It's great."

Laurel smiled. "Thank you." Then, politely she asked, "Do you play an instrument?"

"Oh, not really. Only the drums and tambourine with my uncle Jake's klezmer."

"Klezmer? What kind of an instrument is that?"

Jonathan chuckled. "It's not an instrument. It's a kind of music. Jewish music, from about fifty or a hundred years ago. My uncle found some old music books and records in his basement in Brooklyn, stuff that belonged to his uncle, and he got really excited about it."

Laurel nodded. "What instrument does he play?"

"Oh, lots," said Jonathan. "The clarinet, the guitar, banjo and balalaika and the bazooka . . ."

"Sounds like a weapon," said Laurel, laughing. She had never talked to a boy about music before, never this long, never without feeling hugely embarrassed.

For a moment they stood there just looking at each other. Jonathan still did not move, but began to shuffle his feet, as if he were a battery-charged toy, warming up to a walk.

"When are you guys moving in?" Laurel asked.

"This weekend," Jonathan said. "Was this your room?"

"No. It's my dad's study." Laurel pointed to the many shelves and small cubbyholes where her father had kept his architectural plans.

Jonathan went to the wall, fingering the smooth wooden shelves. "Wow. This is neat. I can keep my models here."

"No, no!" Laurel cried. "You—wouldn't want this room. It creaks. It's not meant to be a bedroom, but an office."

"What do you mean?" Jonathan asked. He suddenly looked like an explorer claiming his territory. "I can have any room I want. My folks don't care. It's our house now," he said.

29

"It's—too cold in here," Laurel said. "Look, this room faces north. It's very uncomfortable, especially in winter. It gets freezing. And there's no heat."

"I like cold rooms," said Jonathan. He stood at the window. "This is neat," he said softly, looking out at the oak tree. The wind chimes tinkled softly. "Are you leaving your chimes here?"

"No! Of course not!" cried Laurel.

Jonathan walked around the room from end to end, as if he were measuring it with his steps. Laurel sat down on the empty window seat, her body a shield between the boy and the wind chimes, the oak, the Unseen.

"I guess I'll put my bed over here," Jonathan said. He stood directly opposite the window, his head outlined by the faded spot where the Chinese brass mirror had hung.

Laurel could hardly gather her thoughts or her breath.

"You should put something there over the faded spot," said Laurel. Her voice sounded stiff, wooden. "Maybe a mirror."

"The spot won't be there," said Jonathan. "We're going to paint the room."

"What color?"

"White."

Laurel felt choked. She turned and walked out.

The boy came after her. "What's wrong? What'd I do? Are you mad?" he called out.

"Jonathan!" The boy's mother suddenly appeared, wearing a crazy T-shirt with a rock-and-roll band of cats pictured on the front. "Jonathan, I need you to help me measure the living room windows. Hello, Laurel."

"Hello, ma'am," Laurel said politely.

"I was thinking," Jonathan's mother said, "we could put a doggie door in the kitchen, use the service porch for the puppy. Then he can go in and out when he needs to."

Laurel blinked. "Puppy? You have a puppy?" The words from the fortune cookie hummed in her mind: *A lean dog shames his master.* "Is—is it a lean dog? Skinny? Or—fat?"

"Neither," said Jonathan's mother. "Jonathan hasn't decided yet on what kind. *I'd* like a cocker spaniel. Do you like dogs?"

Laurel squared her shoulders, took a deep breath, and forced herself to smile. "Oh, I love dogs. Absolutely *love* them." Her mind hummed like a machine—yes, find a way to get over here, in case Great-grandfather refuses to leave. "Maybe," she added breathlessly, "when you get your puppy, I could see it. I'd love to come and see it."

"Well, of course, come over and visit us and the new puppy," said Jonathan's mom. "You can help Jonathan get acquainted with the kids in the neighborhood. You'll both be at the same school. I'll expect to see you here often, Laurel, since you love dogs so much. It's a shame you don't have one of your own."

"I know," Laurel said. She felt her skin tighten like a drum; it always happened when she lied. "But my mother is very allergic to fur."

"What a pity," said Jonathan's mom, and then she drew her son away.

So far, so good, thought Laurel, congratulating herself. She felt very clever, having worked out an excuse to come back to the house. Of course, the consequences were ghastly. She could hardly imagine subjecting herself to a snapping, snarling little beast. It would nip at her fingers, drool on her clothes ... but ...

Laurel reached into her pocket. Her fingers curled around the fortune cookie. Absentmindedly Laurel broke open the cookie and glanced at the fortune. It said: "He who fears the dragon cannot capture the pearl."

She was stunned. Dragon? Pearl?

It meant one must be brave. No gain without risk. She would have to be brave. It would be like entering the dragon's lair, fighting its flaming breath and talons, to capture the treasure, the pearl that the dragon carried under its chin.

That dog of Jonathan's was to be her dragon.

4

*

"The girl plays the flute," Jonathan told Jake a few days later. "She's really good."

"Flute, eh?" said Jake, eyes narrowed and distant.

"Forget it. She plays classical."

"Oh, pardon me," said Jake with a haughty look. "Highbrow."

"When will you come see the house, Jake?" Jonathan asked.

"I'll come when I'm invited."

"I'm inviting you."

Jake gave Jonathan a sad smile. Then he said, "I'm going to barbecue myself some kosher franks for dinner. Want to stay?"

"Sure, I'd love to," said Jonathan. "All we get at my house is tofu and greens." He shuddered.

They walked to the tiny kitchen. Shelves and counters were crammed with food. A portable rotisserie took up most of the countertop.

Jonathan picked up the package of hot dogs. *"Kasher,"* he read in Hebrew.

"Aha," said Jake. "You remember."

"What's not to remember? You taught me when I was four years old. Hebrew's not hard; you just have

33

to imagine the shapes. The *kaf* is like a sideways horseshoe. The *shin* is like a pitchfork. Simple."

"If it's so simple, why won't you make your bar mitzvah?" Jake stood with his hands on his hips, challengingly.

"I don't want to, that's why. It doesn't mean anything. It's just a silly formality."

"Formality? Silly?" Jake clapped his hands to his head. "How can you say such a thing? This is a bar mitzvah I'm talking about, ceremony, a beautiful party, presents."

"That's exactly my mother's point. It's become nothing but a materialistic scam—who needs it?"

"Everyone needs it sooner or later."

"Then I'll get it later."

"Tradition has it, when a boy turns thirteen . . ."

"Spare me," said Jonathan, rolling his eyes. "Look, if my mother doesn't care, why should you? You're the only one bugging me about this. Even Steve . . ."

"Oh, now it's Steve, the big authority on Jewish ritual, is it? Since when did he get so learned?"

"Since he agreed with me that it isn't important," said Jonathan. "Let's eat."

Jake sighed. He turned for one last stab, pointing his finger. "You'll regret this, Jonathan. Someday you'll meet a gorgeous Jewish woman, and it will be important to her."

"Blah, blah, blah," said Jonathan.

"If I didn't outweigh you by a ton I'd punch you," said Jake. He grabbed a huge green head of cabbage and with a sharp kitchen knife began chopping it on his tiny wooden board. He swept the shreds into a bowl with the flat of his hand. "You better call your mom and tell her you're staying. I'll bring you home."

"I've got my bike," Jonathan objected.

He dialed his number. The machine answered with a drum roll, a heavy rock beat. "Yeah! It's us! Leave a message."

Jonathan left a message. "Mom, I'm having dinner with Jake. I'll be home by eight. I've got my bike."

"I'll bring him home!" Jake yelled. "It'll be dark," he told Jonathan, reaching into the refrigerator for mustard and pickles.

"I don't care. I always ride in the dark. I've got a light."

"Your mom doesn't like you taking those streets at night, and I don't blame her," said Jake. He pulled two pickles out of the jar. Pickle juice dripped from his fingers.

"How come you're suddenly so overprotective?" Jonathan asked. "You always say my mom babies me too much, and now . . ."

"Tut-tut-tut," said Jake, shaking his shoulders. It was his way of ending an argument. "Come on, you can set the table."

Jonathan took the blue-and-white plates from the cupboard, brought them to the table in the living room. Something made him turn. "What was that?" he asked.

"What's what?" Jake gave the cabbage another whack. "I don't hear anything."

"Listen!" There were shuffling sounds, a whimper. "What's in there? Why's the bedroom door shut?"

Jake glanced up at the ceiling. "Oh. Well. I didn't want to involve you."

"Involve me in what?" Jonathan moved close to his uncle, and he smelled the moist sharpness of the onions and the savory pickles that were now being chopped on the board.

Jake continued to chop. "Listen, you guys have enough on your minds, with the move and everything. I mean, who needs it? This is my problem. Period."

"What's your problem?" Jonathan had to shout above the sizzling noise as Jake tossed the greens and onions onto a pan and began to stir.

Jake shrugged his massive shoulders. "This mutt that somebody tried to palm off on me. You know, some people really have chutzpah, you know what I mean?"

"Mutt?" Jonathan cried. "You have a dog? In the bedroom? Why didn't you tell me?"

"I'm taking him to the pound tomorrow, that's why." Jake swirled the vegetables in the pan with a long wooden spoon.

"You? Take a dog to the pound? That's ridiculous." Jake never hurt anybody or anything. He'd catch a bee in a dish towel and set it gently out the door rather than swat it.

Jake nodded. "Couldn't go today. I had a rehearsal, and they close at four-thirty."

"Jake, I hope you didn't get me a dog," said Jonathan, suddenly suspicious. "I want to pick out my own dog."

Jake shook the frying pan violently and shouted above the sizzling sounds. "You're nuts. This dog, you couldn't have. You wouldn't want it, believe me. It's the ugliest beast I ever saw. It looks like . . ." Uncle Jake shuddered. "You wouldn't believe it."

"Let me see the dog," Jonathan said.

"No, no, I don't think you should," said Jake, shaking some pepper sauce into his concoction.

"I'm not afraid!" Jonathan yelled. "I've never been afraid of dogs. *Let me at least see it!*"

"See it? You'll faint from shock. Ugly isn't the word for it."

"If it was that bad," Jonathan said, "why did you bring it home?"

"I told you—I had no choice. This guy foisted it on me. First thing tomorrow morning . . ." Jake drew his finger across his throat, like a blade.

"What kind is it, Uncle Jake?" Jonathan asked.

"How would I know?" Jake turned to face him, looking angry. "What do I know about dogs? I grew up in Brooklyn. Who had a dog?"

"Sometimes I can't believe you and Mom grew up in the same family."

"We didn't," said Jake. "By the time your mother was born, I was ten years old. A family is not the same in one decade as in the next. Everything changed," he said gloomily.

As if to accent Uncle Jake's gloom, a long howl rang out and Jonathan rushed to the bedroom door, his uncle following, breathing hard.

Jonathan opened the door. There it was, the ugliest animal Jonathan had ever seen. Mottled and loose-skinned, pink-jowled and panting, the dog raised his bloodshot eyes the moment Jonathan entered and hissed out its greeting in a panting wheeze.

"It's a bulldog," Jonathan whispered, squatting down.

The dog lumbered toward Jonathan. In the next moment Jonathan was flat on the floor, his face an unwilling target for a string of wet, sloppy kisses.

"Uh! Oh! Don't! Stop! Ooh, so wet, *wet*!"

The dog, finished plastering Jonathan's mouth with kisses, tottered over and laid down, its head on Jonathan's foot.

"That dog," said Jake, "obviously thinks you're the king of the world. Look at those eyes!"

And indeed the dog's eyes were focused on Jonathan with a look of pure adulation.

"Okay, Winchester," said Jake, nudging the dog with his toe. "Time to eat."

The dog obliged and followed them to the kitchen.

Jonathan asked, "Why would you name a dog that you were getting rid of tomorrow?"

Uncle Jake pierced several hot dogs with skewers and set them turning on the rotisserie. He poured tomato juice into two large glasses, sliced up a lemon, while Jonathan stood beside him, asking questions.

"Tell me about this dog, Jake. How'd you get him? I better tell you right now, there's no way I'm going to take that dog."

"Tut-tut-tut," said Jake. "I told you. The pound. Tomorrow."

Winchester came over. He sat down, licked his chops.

"The dog is hungry," said Jonathan. "Why don't you feed him?"

"You think I want to get my arm bitten off?"

"Here, let me give him one of those hot dogs," said

38

Jonathan. "He's probably starving. I'll use a paper plate."

Jonathan prepared the plate with meat and bread. The dog sat watching and drooling.

"Here, Winchester." Jonathan set down the paper plate.

The dog sat panting at Jonathan, waiting.

"Good dog," said Jonathan. "Eat."

Instantly the dog pounced on the food. It was gone in a moment. The dog started eating the plate for dessert.

"No!" shouted Jonathan. "Down!"

Instantly the dog flattened, dead. The wagging stump of his tail showed that he was only fooling.

"Let's eat," Jake called. He heaped the hot cabbage onto plates, topped it with hot dogs, and motioned Jonathan to the little table in the living room.

Winchester pulled his bulk over to the table and lay down beside Jonathan's chair. And Jonathan's mind began its chattering. No way, it said, no way am I going to let Jake pull this off. After all, I've never had a dog before, and for years I've been looking in pet stores, at dog books, picking out my dog, deciding, planning. . . . I always wanted a puppy, a cuddly little puppy, soft and sweet. . . . He thinks he's going to get away with this, but I'm not falling for it, not this time, no way.

"So, Sunday's moving day," Jake remarked.

"Yup. The day before school starts."

"Steve likes the house?"

"Yup. Steve likes the house."

Jake dug into his food with gusto. He helped himself to a pickle, then pointed. "Pass the rye bread, please. Isn't this delicious?"

But before Jonathan could reply, a long, rolling belch came from Winchester, a shocking sound that rose from the floor and bounced back off the ceiling.

Jonathan giggled.

Other sounds, incredible rumblings, issued from the dog, together with odors that signaled disaster.

"Out! Out!" cried Jake. "Get him out!"

Holding his breath, Jonathan took Winchester by the collar and led him out through the patio door. He closed the sliding door behind him. Winchester lay down, his great head pressed against the glass, gazing at Jonathan.

No way, Jonathan thought. He chewed his hot dogs and cabbage. It's too big. Too old. Too slobbery. Too smelly.

The dog's lip was pulled back in a look of rapture.

Jake, pointing with his fork, spoke with his mouth full. "The dog loves you."

"I don't love it!" Jonathan yelped. "Who would?"

Jake shrugged. "Beats me."

At last Jonathan sighed and said, "I guess you want me to take this dog to Mill Valley."

Jake looked at him in astonishment. "Who in the world said anything about you? I told you, I'm taking this dog to the . . ."

"Sure, sure," said Jonathan, pushing his plate away. "Where did you get it?"

"Well, it's a long story."

"I like long stories," said Jonathan.

"His master died," said Jake. He took a large handkerchief from his pants pocket and wiped his face. "Yeah. And I caused it."

"That's ridiculous!" Jonathan snapped, aware that his words were clipped, like his mother's. "How could you make the guy die?"

"Well, the old guy was eighty-six, and his son came in from Cincinnati, Ohio, to give him a birthday party. They wanted a klezmer band, so they hired me to do the music, with six pieces, all my favorite instruments, and Abe Krinski on the clarinet."

"So?"

"They had the party at the Burlington Inn, rented the big room upstairs. You should have seen the crowd! Well, the food was up to here, you better believe, with every food known to man and some invented by machine. Before dinner, during, and after dinner, we played. Oh, how we played! Everybody had to dance. I mean, we made their feet tickle, they couldn't stop. So they danced, and the old guy hopped like a grasshopper, like a young buck. It was a sight to see. Hoo! Hoo! Ha! Ha! Ha! You should have seen it, people clapping and shouting and stamping all of them dancing around the old man. You should have seen how happy he was!" Jake groaned. "It was too much for him."

"You mean he . . . ?"

Jake nodded. "May he rest in peace."

"But—but—why did he do it? Why did you? Why did his son . . . ?"

"Questions, questions," said Jake with a wag of his head. "When it's your time, boom! That's it. So, the man died dancing. There's worse deaths, believe me."

"Well . . . what about the dog?" asked Jonathan. He

watched his uncle Jake, the sad rolling eyes, the perspiring forehead, the way Jake's hands and shoulders
and belly moved when he gestured. Something about
Jake seemed similar to the dog.

"The dog belonged to the old guy. Of course, the
son couldn't take it back with him to Cincinnati. He
lives in a little apartment. So the son says, 'Jake, I'll
give you a present, since you were the last person to
make my old papa happy. I'm giving you this wonderful, faithful companion, this purebred and, by the way,
very expensive animal.' So the next thing I know, this
dog is on my doorstep. Brought by a delivery service.
This guy in a uniform comes and brings me the dog.
Says I have to sign here. Imagine! For that face, I
have to sign!"

"When did all this happen, Jake?" Jonathan asked.

"Yesterday."

Jonathan's eyes narrowed. "You never had any intention of taking this dog to the pound, did you?"

Jake pressed both hands to his chest. "I should be
responsible for killing an innocent animal? God for-
bid."

"You know my mom won't go for it," said Jonathan.

"Your mom isn't so bad," said Jake. "Her bark is
worse, as they say, than her bite."

Jonathan pondered. He felt slightly ill, whether
from the cabbage or the shock of Winchester, he
couldn't be sure. Of course, it would be funny, bringing in Winchester when Steve wanted a Dalmatian.
Funny? It would be a major victory. Ever since Steve
had started dating his mom, everything had to be his
way. Tofu burgers. Jogging every morning at six. That

silly punching bag and the stationary bike and all that stuff. Thought he was a jock. Some jock. He was at least forty years old!

He had heard them talking before the wedding.

"He'll get used to the idea," Steve said. "Kids are very adaptable. I should know."

"You'll have to go easy. Don't push him. After all, it's just been the two of us all these years. He won't want to share me."

Laughter. "Nobody wants to share you, doll."

She had met Steve at the record company. He was trying to sell insurance to the executives. It was her job to bounce people. But Steve hung on. He was stubborn.

Usually it was the talent she bounced—and it made her hard. "Sorry, try us again," she would say, her voice a monotone. She never smiled at the people she was bouncing. "It's not our kind of thing," she'd say, looking deadpan. Jonathan knew; he had been to work with her a few times when he was little and she couldn't get a sitter for him.

From somewhere far back in his memory Jonathan remembered a different mom. She was soft and wore a shirt with a lacy collar. She played pretty songs on the recorder and made fancy cookies and smiled a lot. Her goal then was to make records. She loved working with different effects and sound tracks, mixing musical sounds.

Then they moved to Westmont and she got that job at the record company. She started wearing black jeans, weird shirts, and a crystal around her neck. He had watched her change, until she wasn't like his mom at all, but an impostor. Now Steve was hanging on to her all the time, telling her what to eat, when to exercise, where to live, even what kind of dog to get. Well, Jonathan wasn't going to let it go on this way. He was going to fight back, starting today.

"I was going to get a black Lab," Jonathan sighed. "I was going to name him Prince."

"Winchester has pedigree papers," said Jake. "All his shots. Even health insurance." He laughed. "Steve will be glad to hear that."

Jonathan opened the patio door and let the dog in. Winchester sank down on the rug, gazing at Jonathan. His eyes already said it: "Master."

Jonathan sat down on the floor and touched the smooth head. It was warm. He bent down closer. Winchester exuded a certain odor, like greenery and rainwater, also like crackers. It wasn't really bad at all. The dog's back quivered with pleasure under Jonathan's touch.

Uncle Jake pulled on his jacket. "Listen, kiddo, I've got a chess game tonight. So, you want me to load your bike in the car, and you'll take Winchester on the leash?"

"Okay."

"His bed's already in the car," said Uncle Jake, and he went out whistling.

In the week since they had moved, Laurel had had nothing but bad luck. The locker they gave her at school didn't work; she had to stay for an hour after school to get it fixed. By then the bus had left, and Laurel missed her flute lesson. She forgot her math homework. The teacher yelled and cackled and promised her an F for the day.

44

In Chinese school Laurel made the wrong intonation and read: "The scholar bowed down to his old horse."

The children screamed with derisive laughter. Laurel hated them all. That afternoon Laurel had a terrible fight with her mother, ending with Laurel stamping her foot and shouting, "I'm not going back! Never!"

Of course, she had to apologize later.

"I forgive you, Laurel," said her mom. "I know you are nervous about those tryouts. It creates tension."

The next day Laurel realized she did not have her jade necklace. It was just gone. She searched everywhere. No necklace.

She needed all the luck she could get for the Youth Symphony tryouts on Thursday. She needed, quite simply, to find a way to get Great-grandfather back. Without a house spirit to protect her, she was doomed.

The next day Laurel went past Jonathan's locker at noontime.

"Hi!" she said. She smiled.

"Hi," he responded. "How do you like your new house?"

"It's fine," Laurel said. "Do you have your puppy yet?"

"I—well, yeah. I do. Want to to come over and see it?"

"I'd love to," said Laurel.

"How about tomorrow?"

"Perfect," said Laurel. "I'll walk over after my flute lesson." Everything was falling into place. She'd have her flute with her. She'd find a way to get up to the window seat and lure the spirit out.

Obviously, one could not rely entirely on luck; one had to create his or her own good fortune.

Laurel felt very clever and brave.

5

*

Jonathan sat at his desk, trying to study. Homework was piling up. Every night he had two or three pages of math problems to solve, spelling words to learn, English composition papers to write, and for social studies he was supposed to do a research paper titled "My Personal Heritage."

It wouldn't be so bad if he had something to do in between going to school and studying, like back in Westmont. A bunch of the guys used to meet at the grammar school nearly every afternoon and play softball. Then they'd wander over to Curry's in the Center for a fruit pie and a Coke. He hadn't realized how great those days were, with pals like Mickey Greenfield and Eric Flannery and Tom Chubb. And if the guys weren't getting together, there was always Uncle Jake.

Every day after work Jonathan's mom came into his room. She'd stand at the door, watching him with a misty expression on her face, the look that said, "My boy—isn't he sweet? But I worry about him—poor fellow. Is he happy?"

"Hi," she'd say. "What's up?"

"Nothing."

"How was school?"

47

"Okay."

"Do you have a lot of homework?"

"Yeah."

"Need help?"

"No, thanks."

Some conversation. They were stuck; both of them knew it.

"Have you met any boys you like?"

"A couple."

"Oh! Maybe you want to invite someone over for dinner sometime—it's fine with me. Or on Saturday. You and Steve and your friend could go bike riding or . . ."

"Thanks, Mom," Jonathan said, opening another book. She got the hint and left. Then he felt mean for brushing her off.

She was so obvious. Saturdays she worked. Why? It was a trick, to get him and Steve together. He could just imagine them plotting it: If he and Steve were alone in the house, they'd get used to each other, come to like each other, do things like going to ball games and participating in Little League.

Well, he wasn't going to fall for it.

Laurel lay awake. She and her parents had gone out to dinner. Her mother noticed that she wasn't wearing her jade necklace.

"It isn't lost, is it?" Mom asked sharply.

"Of course not," Laurel replied. The lie settled in her throat, like clay. She had no appetite, even for the fortune cookie that came with dessert.

Now she rose from her bed, got the cookie from her

bureau, and broke it open, bending to see it by the faint light from the window.

"Only by cutting is jade given shape."

Jade! A pang shot through her. Coincidence?

Laurel had always felt it; hidden layers of meaning lie all around. Ancestors somehow buzz their past into our ears. The right information comes when we need it, in a cookie, from a palm reader or tarot cards—it doesn't matter, because they are only the vehicle, connecting us to the Unseen.

"Only by cutting is jade given shape." Jade. This fortune was no coincidence. The message was subtle, but definitely meant for her. The very fact that jade was the subject of this fortune, when jade was uppermost on her mind, was electrifying. It was obviously meant to teach her something.

What was it? "Only by cutting is jade given shape." A thing of beauty, Laurel thought, requires effort. Of course, she knew that. Like her flute playing, like trying out for the Youth Symphony.

Perhaps it meant something deeper—that by being changed, we become more beautiful. By suffering we are molded. Yes, that too.

Suddenly Laurel felt light as air, free. Oh, that this should all come to her! She ran on tiptoes to the living room. Maybe Great-grandfather was already here! Spiritman, why should he remain confined in any particular place? It was her own fixation that placed him in the oak tree. He might well have migrated—why not? Then, her bad luck came from some other cause, her own lack of belief, her self-doubts. The fortune could well be Great-grandfather's sign to her. Signs are everywhere. One must know how to read them. That, Laurel knew, was basic.

In the living room she pulled open the drapes. Immediately the room was filled with silvery light.

Moonlight lit the portrait of Great-grandfather, which hung on the wall.

This house had no mantle, so Laurel's mother had placed a table in front of the portrait and set Laurel's golden dragons upon the table on a fine embroidered cloth.

When her grandparents came from China, this would be the spot where they would stand to show their devotion to their ancestor. Bending low to the ground, their foreheads touching the floor, they would give homage to Great-grandfather in a ceremony called kowtowing, which some Westerners found shocking, even amusing. Laurel dreaded the thought of seeing her old grandparents bowing down before a portrait. They would expect her too to behave like a traditional Chinese girl. Laurel shuddered. She reached over and picked up one of the golden dragons and held it close to her chest.

Through the small slit of the window a sudden sharp draft shot out to Laurel's hand. The dragon slipped from her fingers and fell to the floor. Laurel's heart hammered; her knees felt weak. She picked up the dragon in both hands, whispering a prayer for its safety. Even then she could feel the crack with her fingertips. It lay just under the dragon's chin, between two flat curls, a crack about an inch long.

"What's going on?" Laurel's father appeared in his pajamas, peering out at her, holding a flashlight. The beam fell upon Laurel's face.

"I—I—was just visiting my dragons."

Her father came down the stairs and into the room. Gently he touched Laurel's shoulder. "It is time now for dragons—and students—to sleep," he said. He took the dragon from her hands.

Laurel held her breath. He set the dragon down on the table, unsuspecting.

The perfect gift, the gift from Great-grandfather, was flawed now. Every day of her life from now on the crack would be a reproach for her carelessness.

Laurel knocked at the door.

Jonathan answered. Behind him stood a man with shaggy hair and baggy pants, sweating profusely, as if he had been working out. But this man obviously had *never* seen the inside of a gym.

"Hi!" Jonathan said. "This is my uncle Jake—he came over for dinner. First time in our new house. Jake, this is Laurel."

Laurel glanced at the man, big as a volcano, sweating, but seeming pleasant enough.

"I—can come back another day," Laurel said hastily.

"Tut-tut-tut," said Jake, drawing her inside. "Come in. I see you've brought your flute." He nodded at her flute case and backpack stuffed with music. "A musician after my own heart," said he. "Never leave your instrument at home—you never know when you'll want a tune."

Laurel laughed; it came out a little panicked. Where was the dog? Would it simply leap out at her? "I just came from my lesson," she explained. "Thursday are the tryouts for Youth Symphony."

"Are you nervous?" asked Jonathan.

Laurel shook her head. "No. Not really."

Jake nodded vigorously. "Real musicians aren't nervous," he said jubilantly. "Am I right, Laurel? You simply *become* the music—it takes you with it—am I right?"

Laurel nodded. "That's right," she said softly, her cheeks flushed. Actually, she had never discussed this with anybody; she was amazed that someone else knew. She wanted to talk more to this man, to ask him whether he actually *saw* the notes climbing, whirling, merging into colors, as she sometimes did when she was engrossed. Of course she said nothing.

"I guess you want to see Winchester," said Jonathan.

"He's out in the side yard," said Jake. "Where the oak tree is."

All day Laurel had tried to prepare herself. What was she afraid of? The teeth? The claws? The smells of puppy? The way they leapt and wriggled and wouldn't hold still? Did she think she would be eaten by a dog? She couldn't analyze her terror or talk herself out of it. But somehow, now, for the sake of Great-grandfather, she would have to endure.

She hoped the puppy wouldn't jump. Yes, the jumping was definitely the worst part. It made her shudder.

Laurel glanced at Jake. She was glad now that he was here. Such a big man could certainly control a little pup.

"How do you like your new home?" Jake asked pleasantly, not at all in the phony voice some adults use with children.

"It's fine," said Laurel. "We needed more space."

Jake nodded. "I heard. Your grandparents. Bet they'll bring you a present."

Laurel was astonished; she hadn't thought of that. But what could they possibly bring from China that she didn't have here? And what could she possibly want more than what they would steal from her—time with her mother, time alone, and space.

"Did Jonathan tell you about Winchester?" asked Jake.

Jonathan broke in, grinning. "Winchester is the kind of pup who needs no introduction."

It was an odd feeling, walking through the house that had once been hers. The structure was the same, of course, but subtle differences made it seem foreign. People attach parts of themselves to a house, she thought with a sense of shock; it takes on their personalities.

In the kitchen the windows looked different, with pink curtains in place of the sleek blinds Laurel's mother had used. The small desk held eight or ten cookbooks, all vegetarian or "natural," and a telephone in the shape of a duck.

Jonathan opened the back door.

Laurel still gazed back at the counter, on which her mom had kept only a bouquet of artificial flowers, now filled with jars of dried legumes and nuts.

Laurel followed Uncle Jake out the back door.

The next moment everything went into a blur.

Laurel heard sounds. Slurping, straining, wheezing. She felt feelings—a huge muzzle slobbering at her leg, the hot dragon's breath, and the odor of dog, the deepest dog odor she could possibly imagine. She saw teeth, claws, hackles, and an enormous, lolling tongue.

Jonathan, doubled over, clutched at the dog's collar, panting, "He's not exactly a p-p-pup-py!"

Laurel screamed. She hardly felt the rough bark against her knees and face as she scaled the oak tree, her feet scratching off clumps of bark, her hands clawing at branches, until she found herself up on the highest limb, the one outside her father's old study, while below a continuous howling pierced the air.

Never in her life had Laurel climbed a tree or shimmied up a pole or sat up on something high looking down. Her knees trembled. Her hands went numb with the effort of hanging on. Looking down, she swallowed, feeling the emptiness like a sudden deep pit into which she would be plunged any moment.

Uncle Jake reached up, straining and yelling above the mad barking, "Laurel, Laurel, can you get down?"

Laurel closed her eyes. She shook her head. "No," she tried to shout, but the word stuck, came out a whisper, as in a bad dream.

"Is there a ladder in the garage?" Jake shouted to Jonathan.

"No," Jonathan said. "Shut up, Winchester!"

Up in the tree Laurel at last opened her eyes. She looked into the window. The room had been painted white. It was hideous.

"What goes up must come down," shouted Uncle Jake.

Laurel wanted to kill him.

"Can you get down all right?" called Jonathan.

Down? She was starting to feel nauseated. Sour tastes collected in her mouth; her chest seemed to expand, then contract with a strange pressure.

A sharp, sudden crack split the air, like thunder. The branch shook.

Laurel heard the crack, and for an instant, time lengthened, and like a camera she witnessed the entire thing in slow motion—the breaking of the branch, her body falling down, down, rushing down, the crash. The world went on hold. Then the pains began to define themselves—chin, ankle, ribs, mouth.

Laurel heard a groan. Not hers. She felt a wetness on her face, coating her as with varnish, sticky and odorous. She was eye to eye with Winchester, feeling the breath from that huge spotted muzzle into which were tucked two rows of yellow teeth. The tongue retreated only long enough to gather more slime with which to lick Laurel's face.

"Oh! Oh, God!" came the groan from beneath her, and Laurel realized she had landed on top of Uncle Jake.

Jonathan reached out to help her up. "Are you okay?"

"Don't move her! Wait!" groaned his uncle. "Slowly, slowly."

The dog, done with Laurel, began to lap up the uncle.

"Get this dog off me!" shouted Jake.

Jonathan pulled the dog away. "Sit!" he said fiercely.

The dog sat.

"I'm—okay," said Laurel. She stood up slowly and dusted herself off. But her jaw felt strange, as if something under her chin had cracked.

"I can't move," said Uncle Jake. "My leg." Uncle

Jake's body was peculiarly balanced, stuck, one leg twisted behind him, and his hand hanging limp.

"I think I broke some bones," he said, in a tone more curious than pained. Jake pointed to Laurel. "You're bleeding," he said. He reached into his shirt pocket and brought out a handkerchief. "Here, hold this against it."

Laurel realized now that her shirt was bloodstained. Her jaw ached.

"I'll call my dad," Laurel said. "He'll come and take us to the emergency clinic."

Laurel's lips felt curiously numb. She touched the tip of her tongue to her lower lip. It was swollen the size of a walnut.

The fullness of the disaster didn't dawn on her until later, when they were at the clinic. The doctor took seven stitches under Laurel's chin. He gave her a tetanus shot. He prescribed ice packs for her lip. And he told her sternly, "No kissing. You can't pucker. Liquids only for a couple of days, through a straw."

It was Laurel's father who asked the question. "Can she still play the flute?"

The doctor glared. "No way."

"I never heard of such a thing," Laurel's mother scolded. "You could have been killed!"

"Well, I wasn't," Laurel said.

"Don't you sass me! You're a tiger. Wild, always wild and never doing what you're supposed to. What were you doing over there anyhow?"

"I was being polite. I was visiting."

"A boy and a man and a dog? What for? You hate dogs!"

"Leave her be, Jacqueline," Laurel's father said.

56

"Poor girl. She was being brave, being friendly. That tree! We should have cut it down years ago. I feel responsible."

"If she hadn't been up in it, nothing would have happened," said Laurel's mother.

Suddenly her mother shook her head, then she began to cry.

"I'm all right, Mom," Laurel said. The pain in her ribs and under her chin and lips was nothing compared with the ache of disappointment. "I can't play for the tryouts," she whispered. Tears slid from her eyes, flowed down her cheeks.

Her mother's eyes glistened with sorrow. "Poor Laurel," she said softly.

"I just wanted ... you ... to b-be p-p-proud of me," Laurel wept.

"I am proud of you, Laurel," her mother whispered. "Only, sometimes you scare me to death," she said.

Later, Laurel's mom brought her a milk shake, thick and chocolaty, and a straw to drink it with. Laurel's mother sat down gently at the edge of the sofa. She stroked Laurel's hair, and they talked just like old times, and her mother sang softly, the old songs Laurel had loved when she was little. After a time Laurel's mom tiptoed out and Laurel lay on the sofa alone.

She gazed at the twin golden dragons as they stood beneath the portrait of Great-grandfather. Then she realized that the cut under the chin of the dragon exactly matched her own.

She wished she could tell her mother everything, and she almost called out. But as Laurel gazed at the gilded dragons they became suddenly menacing, accusing. Their smiles seemed malicious now, and their posture suggested attack.

Spirits, Laurel thought, can get angry too. They can be vicious. What else could have made such a horrible thing happen?

6

✳

"I'd better call my folks," said Jonathan when they got home, "and prepare them."

"Good idea," said Jake.

But they had already left their jobs and were on the way home. As soon as he heard the car, Jonathan went to the door.

"Don't come in! Don't come in!" he shouted.

"What's the matter with you?" yelled his mom. "Of course we're coming in."

"Let me tell you first," Jonathan pleaded. "Jake is here. He had a little accident, and I don't want you to be scared, or anything, when you see him, but he . . ."

They burst in the door. On the sofa with crutches beside him, his left ankle in a cast, right wrist bandaged, and a patch over his right eye, sat Jake, smoking a cigar.

"Jake! Jake!" Jonathan thought his mother would pass out. She wrung her hands, sighed, cried, scolded, finally sat down on the sofa beside her brother, while Steve went to the window to examine the broken tree.

Jonathan and Jake had to explain over and over. "It's only a sprained wrist and a broken ankle," said Jake grandly, "nothing to get upset about."

"What about your eye?" cried Mom.

"Just a little scratch from a twig," said Jake.

Steve went to the window. "We've got to take that tree down," he said. "Why did Laurel climb up?"

"Beats me," said Jonathan. "I think she was trying to get away from Winchester."

"That's ridiculous," said his mom. "The girl loves dogs, she told me so."

Steve rubbed his chin, frowning. "Jake, there's no way you can stay alone in that apartment and take care of yourself. We want you to stay with us, Jake. Don't we, Marion?"

"Of course," said Jonathan's mother. "He can sleep in with Jonathan."

She glanced at Jonathan, a mixture of tenderness and doubt. The look said it clearly: "This is what you've always wanted, Jonathan. Now you've got it."

That morning at exactly sixteen minutes after six by Jonathan's clock, the rattling started. It was as though an invisible giant were shaking the door, making it quiver from top to bottom. Vibrations echoed through the room; it was like a shot of electricity, swift and violent, and just as quickly it vanished.

Jonathan sat up. There on the other side of the room, bulky in the small twin bed and bunched up under his covers, lay Jake. Jake's instruments spilled out from the corners. Stuff lay in cardboard boxes. On Jonathan's desk were piled Jake's stamp albums, catalogs, songbooks, and various drafting tools.

Jake had spent the entire dinner patting his pockets and fretting about his albums and his instruments.

"Somebody could break in and steal them—what would my life be worth then?" Jake had demanded.

"More than it is now," Jonathan's mom retorted. "You'd be a hundred times better off without all that junk. It only weighs you down."

But Steve had said quietly, "I know how he feels, Marion. I'll take him back for his things."

So Steve had gotten Jake into the car, and they drove all the way across the bridge, through the city, and to Colma. By the time they got back, Jonathan was asleep. Now he saw the result. Overnight Jonathan's room had been transformed.

Uncle Jake let out a snore, long and rattling.

Quietly Jonathan got out of bed and went to his worktable. He cleared off Jake's jacket and card file and small stack of music magazines.

Only yesterday afternoon, before Jake had arrived, Jonathan had sat here at this table, working on Mogul the Muscle Man.

It was a terrific model, about a foot and a half tall, a dark gray blue, like human flesh seen by night. It had occurred to Jonathan that the head could be bigger, to do justice to Mogul's burly back and shoulders.

Jonathan often modified his models; he had hung a tiny plastic heart, originally from a Cracker Jack box, inside his Scorpio the Skeleton Man. He glued hair, cut from his own head, to Ivan the Inner Man. For Mogul the Muscle Man he made a larger, better face, with large, lidless eyes that gave him a rather vacant, monstrous look, and fleshy lips and a broad forehead. Using a pin, Jonathan then inscribed a fancy version of the letter *M* onto Mogul's forehead.

Now Jonathan surveyed his handiwork. Mogul the Muscle Man was nearly done. Somehow in the move a small piece had broken from the man's chest, right

61

where the heart would be. Carefully Jonathan tore a small piece of clay from a lump he kept in plastic wrap. He worked the clay until it was smooth and pliable, then he fashioned an organ to fit perfectly over the hole.

For a moment Jonathan allowed himself to slip back into the old fantasy of the perfect father, a blend of Superman and a baseball pro and the dad with the curly hair that he vaguely remembered. How could the right dad ever come along if Steve kept hanging around? And how could he get rid of Steve?

Jonathan's stomach felt knotted, and his hands were clenched into fists. If only he had the strength, the power . . . to what? To get rid of Steve. Fight him. Scare him away. Anything.

Jonathan looked down at Mogul the Muscle Man. The patch and the new face made him look tough and powerful. If only he were real, Jonathan thought. If only Mogul the Muscle Man could move in and do battle for him. . . .

"Go for it," Jonathan whispered. "Get rid of Steve." Then he set his model on the shelf to dry.

Laurel waited for her mother to come home. All day she had thought of nothing else but the fêng shui man. Mr. Wu was a trained professional. He had spent his life trying to understand the forces of nature and helping people to live in harmony with them. He knew all about unseen spirits and what they can do to a person, for good or evil. Surely Mr. Wu would understand Laurel's problem with Great-grandfather Lin Peng.

It seemed almost unbelievable that the chain of events that began with selling the house had led to this moment, the complete destruction of everything Laurel had dreamed about for the past two years. In an instant it had all been shattered.

If only, she thought, if only she hadn't lied to Jonathan about loving dogs. If only she hadn't gone over there. If only she hadn't scaled the tree, if the branch hadn't broken, if . . . on and on and on.

It was more than a week since the accident. Her lip was healed. Still she had not touched her flute.

Miss Windemann had telephoned to see about her lessons. "I'm not ready yet," Laurel told her.

Laurel's father stood in the doorway. "Laurel," he called, "it's not like you to give up your lesson. I'm afraid you are going to fall far behind if you don't practice, and once that happens—I hate to see you lose all the work you've done."

"What good is it?" Laurel burst out. "All I do is play with the dumb school orchestra—have you heard the baby pieces we have to play?"

"It's just for another year," her father said gently. "Try to hang in there."

"Just a year," Laurel muttered. Didn't he understand that a year was like forever?

She hadn't the heart to play here in this new house. Somehow the new rooms were not receptive to her music, the house did not embrace the melodies, but left them disjointed, cold.

Now in her room Laurel took her flute out of the case. She put the pieces together, lifted the instrument to her lips, and gently blew.

But the notes wavered and fell, lightweights, to the floor.

She lay the flute down and sat at her desk, opened

63

up her embroidered satin box where she had placed all her fortunes. She lay out the last three fortunes, in the order received.

"A lean dog shames his master."

"He who fears the dragon cannot capture the pearl."

"Only by cutting is jade given shape."

Each of the fortunes, she now saw, was a prediction of the future, a warning.

The first told her she would meet a dog and its master.

The second foretold an encounter with a beast, guardian of something valuable.

Third, the fortune about the jade and cutting.

Now Laurel fingered the cut under her chin. That too had been forewarned. The jade was she, herself, smooth and pretty—yes, everyone said so. But she was selfish and mean, unwilling to accept her old grandparents into the house. She had to be taught a lesson, had to suffer, be denied her dearest wish, the Youth Symphony.

She thought of her own cowardice, predictable and predicted. Her fear of the dog had defeated Laurel's plan, to entice the ghost to come with her. Instead she had invaded its home. It had taken revenge by tossing her out of the tree.

All clear and predictable, when you knew how to read it. But—would he? Would a kind and generous house spirit, the spirit of Great-grandfather, ever cause her harm?

Laurel did not know. It took an expert to determine such fine points. She had to see Mr. Wu.

* * *

64

Laurel waited until after dinner, when her mother sat with a cup of tea, browsing through the evening paper.

Laurel sat beside her, watching her mother's face. Sometimes she could tell from the slightest flickering of her mother's eye, the smallest movement of her mouth or nostrils, exactly how her mother felt.

Now her mother was tired. Concerned. A little tense.

"Mom," she said softly. "I want to ask you something."

Her mother glanced up, a swift gesture. "Yes?"

Nervously Laurel broke open a fortune cookie and quickly read it. "An empty vessel can be refilled."

Wordless, Laurel handed the fortune to her mother, who read it and nodded. "True," said her mother, nothing more. "I think it means that a thing has many uses."

"Or that you shouldn't give up, when something you had seems empty."

"What did you want to ask me, Laurel?"

"I think we should call the fêng shui man to come over. After all, we've had nothing but bad luck."

Her mom said nothing, but her eyes were suddenly lively, and she seemed ready for action.

"Bad luck?" She pondered, nodding slowly. "Yes. You falling out of that tree, then missing the Youth Symphony tryouts." She took a sip of her tea. "Two things," she said. "Not conclusive."

Laurel took a deep breath. "I did not tell you the whole truth," Laurel said with a heavy sigh. "My jade necklace is gone. I lost it somehow when we were moving. I've searched everywhere."

"I see. Three things, then," she said.

"Yes," said Laurel.

"We'll see," said her mother. "Mr. Wu has moved. But I'm sure I've got his number somewhere." Her mother's fingers drummed on the table, and Laurel's heart sank.

"I think we should call him right away," she said. "Anything could happen. Before your parents come, I mean."

Her mother gave Laurel a sharp glance. "How come you are so concerned, suddenly, about your grandparents? Laurel, I am not used to falsehood from you. Is anything else the matter? Anything I should know?"

"No, nothing," said Laurel.

She thought of the golden dragon, flawed, as she herself surely was.

It happened the next day and the next. At exactly sixteen minutes after six in the morning Jonathan's door shivered violently from top to bottom, sounding like sheet metal being shaken by a ferocious wind.

"It's only the pipes," Jonathan's mother told him when he complained. "It's the aftermath of Steve's shower."

But Steve didn't shower until seven in the morning. Why were they trying to con him?

Now Steve came jogging into the kitchen. "Hey!" he called cheerfully to Jonathan. "I've signed us up for the ten-K race. They're giving away neat sweatshirts."

"I don't jog," said Jonathan.

Jonathan's mom said, "Well, maybe you'll change your mind. It's a gorgeous shirt, with a city emblem

66

on it. I bet all the kids from your school will turn out."

Steve added, "I saw some nice looking girls when I was signing up—I think they even live on our street."

Jonathan poured himself some cereal. "Thanks," said Jonathan. "But no thanks."

Steve turned on the juice machine. It hummed and jiggled, sucking in pieces of carrot and celery and beets as Steve pushed them into the slot.

"Hey, Jonathan," said Steve. "Tonight I'm setting up the punching bag in the back room. You can use it too."

Jonathan ate his cereal. He yelled above the whir of the machine. "Don't you guys hear that shaking in the morning? Am I the only one?" The machine stopped; Jonathan was still screaming.

His mother sat down, facing Jonathan. "Okay. I did mention it to Sabrina, my yoga teacher. She thinks it's a poltergeist. A playful ghost."

"Mom, a poltergeist? Like in some stupid movie?"

"Where did she get that idea?" asked Steve, handing a glass of juice to Jake, who nodded his thanks. Since his arrival less than a week ago Jake had lost three pounds.

"Well, Sabrina said it happens sometimes, especially when there's a blossoming teenager in the house."

Jonathan felt things crowding in on him. Jake, Steve, and his mother—they were all staring at him. "Come on, Mom, now you're saying it's my fault?"

"It's not your *fault*," said his mom. She stuck the

tofu crisps into the microwave oven and punched in the time.

"According to Sabrina," continued Mom, "sometimes these—uh—changes attract capricious spirits. Poltergeists are common when there is an adolescent in the house." She pointed at Jonathan. "Like you."

Beep. The microwave oven sounded, and his mom brought out the strips, colored pink and yellow to resemble bacon.

Jake popped several of the flat strips into his mouth and crunched meditatively. "Not bad. If you like roasted cardboard."

"They're also lean," said Jonathan's mother, "and healthy. Which is more than can be said for some people I know."

"You're saying I make that door shake?" Jonathan persisted. "How?"

"Your emerging ... ah ... manhood," said his mom with a grin.

Jake and Steve laughed.

Furious, Jonathan went upstairs. Winchester, breathing heavily, lay at the head of the stairs, the place he had claimed for himself ever since the tree accident. Once Winchester was settled nothing could move him, neither threats nor promises.

"Hardly my idea of a sporting dog," Steve had said when Jonathan first brought him home. "But there's one thing I know. A boy's relationship with his dog is sacred."

He had to be kidding. Sacred? But Steve looked dead serious. Later Jonathan heard him saying to Mom, "Of course I thought Jonathan would have a lot more fun with a Dalmatian or an active breed."

"You're an active breed yourself," Mom had said, laughing, and Jonathan knew they'd be kissing again.

Now Jonathan sat down beside Winchester, and he gently stroked the dog's head. The dog flicked his ears. "I hate the way the three of them laugh at me," Jonathan said.

Winchester licked Jonathan's hand.

"He's not my father!" Jonathan said.

Winchester grunted, then sighed.

"He thinks that by being nice to Jake, he'll butter me up. He thinks by giving Jake carrot juice and tofu everything will be cool. Well, it isn't!"

The dog whimpered. Jonathan leaned over and kissed Winchester lightly on the forehead. "You're the only person I can really talk to," he whispered. Winchester thumped his tail, ecstatic.

Jonathan went into his room and sat down at his worktable. He looked at all his completed projects standing in a row. Now they gave him no satisfaction.

Manhood, emerging manhood. Jonathan wanted to punch something—but he'd be darned if he was going to punch Steve's stupid punching bag in the extra room! Steve had been fixing up that room for weeks, with posters and his rowing machine and stationary bike. He and Mom worked out, and they played records and laughed.

"Come on, Jonathan!" Steve would yell, sounding all peppy, like some kind of a big-league football coach. "Join us!"

They didn't really want him. Why would they?

He wasn't a little kid. He wasn't an idiot. He knew his mom and Steve had sex. Not that he cared. Why would he care?

He'd read plenty of magazines and that junk they distribute at school, with the corny sketches and medical-sounding words. It was something to laugh about with the other guys, to act uninterested about. Until a guy was alone, and things got weird.

Early in the mornings, and sometimes during the day, Jonathan's voice took on a kind of croak. He was hungry all the time—hungry in a different way, as if there were a huge vacuum in his stomach, and that wasn't all. He would sweat with the least exertion, and he'd dig through his mom's medicine shelves looking for deodorant, and then she'd yelled at him, "What do you want, Jonathan? What are you looking for?" But he was too embarrassed to tell her. He found himself thinking thoughts that seemed to barge into his brain completely uninvited. He bumped into things; his hands were growing too large for his arms. And that was only the part that showed. The rest of it was too awful to mention.

Of course, if his dad had lived, things would be different. They'd talk. A dad wasn't like a pal or an uncle—you could tell a dad anything.

The thought sent a slow, burning pain through Jonathan's body. He had hardly any memories, only two, saved like pictures in his mind, which he seldom took out, afraid they might become worn and disappear.

One was of a curly-haired man holding out his arms in the bathtub, and little Jonathan being placed on his chest in the warm water, and giggles and tickles, the blue-and-white plastic boat bobbing on the water, and Dad making motor noises, *bubb-bubber-bbub-bub*.

The other picture was the three of them walking along a path in a park with willow and acacia trees, and Jonathan eating his first Eskimo Pie, amazed at the delicious delight of it, chocolate and cool vanilla and nuts all together, and then Dad carrying him on his shoulders so that he could see up into the trees. He spotted a bird's nest and pointed and shrieked and clapped his little hands, not knowing the word for it, and Dad stopped and looked and then he smiled and gave Jonathan a big hug and said, "Wow! That's a bird's nest, Jonathan! A bird family lives there in the tree, just like you and Mommy and me live in our house."

Now Jonathan gazed out the window at the oak tree and the gash left by the severed limb. It was somehow like a body, maimed and torn, hurting. "I know just how you feel," Jonathan whispered.

A thin voice wafted back, a faint hissing, almost like the wind between the dry leaves. "Kindred spirits," came the sigh. "Broken things can be mended."

It was not the first time Jonathan had sensed something from the tree. Noises, impressions seemed to surge toward him, a gentle hiss, a sigh or a moan. He had pushed it out of his mind. People who hear trees talking are nuts, no doubt about it.

Jonathan got dressed for school. From downstairs he heard Steve and Jake and his mother laughing.

I got what I wanted, he thought bitterly, surveying the mess in his room—Jake's wet towel on the floor, Jake's crumpled blankets on the extra bed, Jake's instruments and music books and catalogs scattered everywhere, and worst of all, Jake in the kitchen with Steve and his mother, and they were having the time of their lives, laughing.

A long, disjointed snore came from the hall.

Winchester.

When Mom first saw Winchester that night, Jonathan thought she'd collapse. She looked from Jake to Jonathan and back, saying, "Something is going on here—I don't know what. Okay. It's your decision, Jonathan, I'm not about to go back on my word. But I'll tell you one thing, you are responsible for this dog."

Jonathan picked up his backpack and jacket and stepped carefully over the dog. "Bye, Winchester," he said.

What he couldn't figure out was why Laurel had lied to him. She was obviously terrified of dogs. Why had she told him just the opposite?

It rained that night, with thunder and lightning ripping across the sky and fierce torrents of water bombarding the roofs and the windows.

Outside, the oak tree seemed to groan and heave, like a dying man. Branches slapped across the windowpane. Jonathan twisted and turned in his bed.

Jonathan turned on his side, facing the shelf where Mogul the Muscle Man stood. Outlined against the crashing thunderbolts that tore across the sky, the shadow of Mogul the Muscle Man stretched up hugely on the back wall. It seemed for a moment that Mogul the Muscle Man's muscles actually rippled, that his fist was clenched. It seemed for an instant that the fist raised itself and came crashing down with such force that the house shook.

Jonathan heard a shattering, splintering sound from downstairs. From the hall came a shout, then a terrible clatter and thud.

Jonathan leapt up. Jake followed, hobbling on his crutches, yelling out, "What's the matter? Are you okay, Steve?" Jonathan's mother already stood at the head of the stairs, where Winchester lay, immovable. Her hands were clasped to her cheeks, and she looked white as a ghost.

At the bottom of the staircase, all in a heap, lay Steve.

7

*

"For a modern woman, Jacqueline, you are remarkably superstitious," said Laurel's father.

It was Saturday morning; they waited out on the front porch for the fêng shui man, Mr. Wu.

"Better to be safe than sorry," said Laurel's mom. "I should have had Mr. Wu come out right away, even before we bought the house."

"Now, Jacqueline," said Laurel's dad, "I thought you were already an expert on luck and the placement of things."

"Don't tease," said Laurel's mom with a shake of her head. "It doesn't pay to offend. . . ."

"Speaking of paying, what is Mr. Wu going to charge us for this?"

"Look, Frank, all things are not measured with money," retorted Laurel's mother. "Remember the time we almost bought that house in the canyon? If it hadn't been for Mr. Wu . . ."

"The place was overrun with termites," said Laurel's father. "And the plumbing was rotted out."

"Exactly my point," said Laurel's mom with an emphatic nod.

The small, dark blue car came into view.

"There he is!" exclaimed Laurel.

He was a small man, precise and neat, with carefully groomed hair and mustache. He wore a dark gray business suit and he carried a briefcase.

After the greetings were over, Mr. Wu walked back to the curb, and with pad and pencil in hand, surveyed the lay of the land.

Laurel watched him from afar. The fêng shui man threw back his head and squinted his eyes. From the contours of the land, Mr. Wu derived important clues to the subterranean spirits that influenced the occupants above.

Having surveyed the exterior, Mr. Wu came back onto the porch where Laurel stood waiting.

"Good morning, Laurel," he said, nodding.

Laurel ducked her head in respect. "Good morning, Mr. Wu. How is everything?"

"It appears satisfactory," said Mr. Wu, "so far. One must not jump to conclusions. Is there water behind that clump of trees?"

"A dry creek bed," Laurel replied.

"Dry," repeated the man. "Hmm." He made a note. "It would be better if it were flowing," he said. "This bush," he pointed with his pen, "has to be cut down. It blocks the light and air from the window; luck can get caught in the brambles. What room is that?" He pointed again.

"My father's study."

"Ah. Well. We must tell him immediately. Let us go inside."

Laurel lead the way. At the door Mr. Wu stopped, and his face burst into a broad smile. "The house number!" he exclaimed.

"Three nine zero," said Laurel, smiling back. "I know. It's very lucky, isn't it?"

"Very," said the fêng shui scholar with a last glance at the outside before he went in. "And yet your mother said something about having had problems." Mr. Wu swung the door open and shut several times, murmuring, "This door has to be rehung, so that it will open from left to right, not right to left. That way the wind will not enter so sharply when the door is opened."

"Would that create bad luck?" Laurel asked.

"Of course it could," said Mr. Wu. "But it's not so simple. There are many influences. Including the occupants themselves." He smiled. "Unfortunately, many people forget that they play the greatest role in their own destiny, and they blame the spirits, or the fêng shui man." He sighed, but not sadly; Mr. Wu seemed always hopeful.

Now Laurel lowered her voice to a whisper. "Mr. Wu, I need to ask you something."

"Ask!" The man frowned, already concentrating.

Laurel chose her words carefully. "When there is a spirit in the house, and it is an old spirit, an ancestor, how can it be made to move?"

The man put his fingertips to his lips. His eyebrows sprang together, so that thick folds of flesh hooded his eyes. "Ah, that is difficult," he said with a sigh. "Once a spirit attaches itself to a house it will not usually move, except to—ah—disappear altogether. Is this what you had in mind, child?"

"No! No!" cried Laurel, aghast. "I only wanted him to move with us. You see, since we have left the old house I have had very bad luck."

Mr. Wu nodded. "I understand. You have a—uh—relationship with this house spirit."

Laurel nodded, then used her mother's word. "Exactly," she said.

"I see," he said, stroking the corners of his mouth with his thumb and forefinger. "How about the new owners? Have they had any—ah—encounters with this spirit? Has there been any uneasiness? Strange events, sounds, stirrings—you know. Dangers?"

"No," said Laurel. "At least, I don't think so." She shifted and cleared her throat. "Well, actually, I did go over there and I fell out of the tree." Laurel lifted her chin so that the fêng shui man could see her scar. "Of course, I can't say that everything that happens is the fault of the spirit. As you said, it could be me. Or them."

"Them?"

"The new family. Maybe they have antagonized . . ."

"Could be. Are they Chinese?"

"No. Jewish."

"Well, I know that Jewish people sometimes have their own ways of consecrating a house. They put prayers on the doorpost. Have they asked you for help?"

"No," she replied. Laurel looked directly into the fêng shui scholar's eyes, and she felt a depth of kindness there. "What I really wanted to do was to bring the house spirit here with me. I tried to entice it to come out."

"How?"

"With my flute."

"Ah! Very interesting. It likes your music?"

77

Laurel nodded. "I think so. But I was interrupted. It didn't work."

"If at first you don't succeed," said Mr. Wu, "try, try again." He grinned and giggled. "Old Chinese proverb."

Laurel's mother came to the doorway. "Laurel! Don't disturb Mr. Wu. Let him do his work."

"Nearly finished, Mrs. Wang!" called the fêng shui man. "Laurel is no trouble—she is quite a delightful young girl."

He turned once again to Laurel, his face serious. "I trust your parents do not know about this spirit."

Laurel nodded.

"Your secret is safe with me," he said softly. "I must warn you. If you do disturb the spirit, you take a risk. Once it is cut loose, so to speak, there is a danger. It might cause disruptions, you know, pranks and disturbances. Or, he might decide to . . ." the fêng shui expert waved his hand, "keep on going. Vaporize. Disappear."

"Laurel!" her mother called again, hands braced in the doorway. "Are you ready for Chinese school? We have to leave in a few minutes."

"Yes, Mother."

Vaporize. Disappear. Cause disturbances.

Laurel felt ill, shaky. The one thing she had really wanted to know, she had not been able to ask. And that was, Why? Why would Great-grandfather's spirit suddenly turn against her like this?

"I—I'm not sure I can take that risk," said Laurel.

"Then the only other choice is to visit him where he resides," said the man, "and be willing to share him."

"Share him!" exclaimed Laurel. Such an idea had not entered her mind. "You mean—with someone else?"

"Exactly." The man smiled.

Anger clouded Laurel's brain—she wanted to stamp her foot and shout, "Never! Never!"

But she made her face placid and she smiled politely and even dipped her head down in respect.

Jonathan jolted awake in the middle of the night. He almost shouted. A beam of light from his lantern fell fully upon his face.

The lantern stood on Jonathan's bureau, shining of its own volition.

"Jake!" he called out.

"Whatsamatter?" Jake answered groggily.

"Are you doing that?"

Jake groaned, pulled himself up, and swung his leg, encased in the plaster cast, out onto the floor and sat rubbing his face, confused. "Why is that light on?"

"I thought you turned it on."

"Not me. It happened last night too. Aimed straight at me. I got up and turned it off."

"Isn't that weird? Like the door shivering, the vase falling off the pantry shelf, Steve getting knocked down the stairs like that . . ."

"Sounds like a golem," said Jake, his voice hollow.

"What's a golem?"

Jake put on the light. Instantly the room seemed friendly again. Jake pulled himself up and hobbled across the room, turned off the lantern, opened the back, and dumped out the batteries. "There. At least that's settled. A golem," he said, moving awkwardly back, "is a sort of ghost from Transylvania or Poland or Germany—he seems to turn up all over the place. In the Middle Ages, you know, people—some people—thought the ultimate in delight would be to create a person."

"You're kidding."

"Not at all," said Jake. He sat down heavily on Jonathan's bed. His pajamas were rumpled, like his hair and his cheeks. He exuded a warm, friendly smell.

"What was the golem made of?" Jonathan asked.

"Oh, spare parts, I suppose. Stuff and junk." He chuckled, coughed. "Like your model." Jake pointed to Mogul the Muscle Man. "An android, with life breathed into him by some kind of magic. I don't know the whole story. But there's one thing I know . . ."

Jonathan noted that Jake was sounding like Steve. He shuddered.

"Yes? What's that?"

"The golem got too strong for his own good and had to be destroyed."

Jonathan blinked. It had always been impossible to tell whether Jake's stories had any basis in fact, or whether they all relied on his imagination. "It sounds more like a monster than a ghost," he said.

"True," said Jake. "Sort of the Frankenstein's monster idea. The fellow comes alive. He is very powerful, and he follows orders. But sometimes he goes berserk. The problem is, he has no brains and no soul."

Lunchtime was nearly over. Jonathan had spent most of the hour looking for Laurel, after gulping down a taco and an apple turnover. He had not seen Laurel since the accident.

In the car on the way home he realized she was not crying about her injury, but about missing tryouts for the Youth Symphony.

At last he found her sitting on a bench with three other girls. One was in his homeroom class, Polly Stenson. He had seen the other two girls before, walking home from school. He knew their names. They were Rachel and Rita, and one was cuter than the other. He heard the guys talking about them, trying to decide who was the cutest, tall Rachel with those big brown eyes and terrific build, or short Rita, with soft red hair and dimples, always laughing. That was the problem. They were always laughing, talking, goofing off with some guy or other walking them home. Jonathan never even had a chance to say "hi."

Now he called out, "Hi, Laurel!"

All the girls turned around and looked at him. He felt like a toad on display. Suddenly he forgot how to speak.

"These are my friends," said Laurel. "Rachel, Rita, and Polly. This is Jonathan. His folks bought our house."

Jonathan marveled at how Laurel could pull this off—he never knew how to introduce people, stumbling over whose name came first, who everybody was.

"Hi, hi, everybody," said Jonathan. He smiled. Rita gave him a grin, and all he could think about for the next several moments were those dimples.

"You live on the same street we do," said Rachel.

"I live in the white-and-blue house on the corner. Rita lives a block farther down."

"I've seen you there," said Jonathan. He worked over several ideas in his mind, gazing up as if he were looking for a cue card—what came next?

Fortunately the bell rang. The girls scooped up their stuff and waved. "Bye, Jonathan!" they said in chorus, and they all giggled.

He managed to grab Laurel by the arm. "Wait a minute, Laurel. I've got to talk to you."

The other girls went on, whispering and laughing, and Rita glanced back at him twice.

"I've been wanting to talk to you," Jonathan said in a low voice. "Weird things are happening at the house," he said, "like the way that branch broke. Jake is staying with us now."

She stopped walking and turned to stare at him. "So?"

"It was what I wanted," Jonathan said miserably. "Don't you see?"

"I don't see what's so weird," Laurel said.

"Well, first of all, the tree. It . . ." Jonathan took a deep breath. "It seems to . . . well . . . it talks."

Laurel seemed to freeze, and her cheeks turned bright red, as if she'd been struck.

"It—talks," she repeated. "Jonathan, trees don't talk," she said. "Maybe it's the wind."

"I know it sounds crazy! But listen," he said, walking rapidly now, for Laurel was running ahead of him. "Listen! It's not just the tree. Lights go on and off in the night. The bedroom door shivers and shakes. And Steve fell down the stairs and nearly killed himself."

82

They were at the building; nearly all the kids were inside by now.

"We'll be late for class," said Laurel.

"Laurel! Come over and see for yourself," Jonathan said.

"I've got a lesson this afternoon."

"Come after the lesson," he said. "Okay? Come and see Winchester. He's been depressed ever since the accident. Really, you should come and see him."

Laurel nodded. "Okay," she said, and hurried in to her class.

"Does your lip still hurt?" asked Miss Windemann.

"No. I'm fine," said Laurel.

"Then perhaps your mind is on something else," said the flute teacher. "Let's call it a day." The teacher got up, sighed, and when Laurel stood at the door ready to leave, Miss Windemann put her hand momentarily on Laurel's shoulder.

"Laurel," she said, "don't let your disappointment overshadow your goals. Next year you will be that much better prepared for the Youth Symphony. Who knows, this might have been the best thing for you. Sometimes," she added, "we just have to trust fate."

"Yes, Miss Windemann," said Laurel, an automatic response. She did not need more philosophy. What she needed was action. What she needed was power.

She walked quickly toward the house that now belonged to Jonathan's family—it was difficult to realize it wasn't hers anymore. Wind blew her hair into her face and whipped about the branches of trees. She had never liked wind, the way it made the chimes clatter and scream, as if they were angry.

83

Laurel recalled the last fortune, and as she walked she said it aloud, like a mantra. "An empty vessel can be refilled, an empty vessel can be refilled, refilled, refilled."

The meaning of that last fortune was crystal clear: The empty vessel was her flute. It had many uses—orchestra, symphony, and yet another use, it could lure out a ghost. Mr. Wu had agreed. Now everything was fitting together.

She would have to be tactful and clever. Find a way to get upstairs alone, sit in the window seat, and with her flute entice Great-grandfather's spirit out of that tree.

There was no use denying it; Laurel had hovered all her life between believing and pretending to believe.

But now that Jonathan had experienced the ghost, there was no longer any doubt of its reality.

8

*

A clamor greeted Laurel even as she came up the walk. It was rock music coming from the downstairs room, punctuated with dull thumps and rattling sounds. Laurel's parents had used that room as a den. Now, evidently, it had been turned into a gym. At last, during a break in the action, Laurel rang the bell.

Jonathan appeared, looking startled, then he smiled. "Hi. Come on in."

Laurel stepped inside. Plants swooped down from the mantle, long tendrils nearly touching the floor. Records and discs and musical paraphernalia were everywhere. Her mother would never have allowed such clutter. Laurel stared, amazed and fascinated.

"How is your dog?" Laurel asked politely. She peered about, expecting to find the dog hiding behind Jonathan, ready to pounce.

"He's a little depressed, actually," said Jonathan.

"Where is he?"

"He likes to hang out upstairs. Right at the top of the stairs. It's weird."

No, it's not, Laurel wanted to say; she knew that dogs were sensitive to spirits. The top of the stairs was the very place where the wind blew softly, carrying the gentle spirit vibes through the hall.

85

"Want to put your stuff down?" Jonathan offered.

"No, thanks," Laurel said. In her backpack was her flute; she felt secure with it on.

The sounds from below accelerated—bam! Bam! Bubububububam!

"What is that?" Laurel asked.

"Punching bag. Steve."

"I want to talk to you," Laurel said. She lowered her voice. "You said something about the tree talking." She kept her face molded, devoid of emotion.

Jonathan chewed his lip, scraped his foot. "Well, I wouldn't exactly say it talks. More like humming. Actually, it's more a feeling than a sound. Although I . . . um . . . do have the impression of words, like it said to me, 'kindred spirit.' "

He was miserable; Laurel could see it in his eyes.

"Things have been happening," Jonathan continued. "Every morning exactly at six sixteen, my door goes into this—well, it's like a fit. It rattles and shakes. I told my mom. She just sort of laughs and says it's a poltergeist. They all don't take it seriously. If I keep after them, I know what will happen. My mom will send me to a shrink. I don't want to go to any stupid shrink."

"Why would they send you to a shrink?"

"Well, I suppose if you hear talking trees, most people would think you are nuts."

"I don't."

"You—don't? Do you mean you've heard it too?"

"I mean, sometimes there are vibes in a house," Laurel began. She really didn't want to say more. Why reveal her personal life? Her ghost was nobody's business.

86

"Sometimes I feel as if—you know . . ." Jonathan lowered his eyes and his voice, "like something in it is alive."

Laurel said nothing, and she kept her face impassive.

Jonathan's voice cracked; he looked flushed and embarrassed. "Sometimes when I go to the window," he whispered, "I feel as if something is out there, watching. And sort of—growing."

Laurel felt a tightening, like a band around her throat. She only nodded.

"When Uncle Jake got hurt, it seemed pretty natural, you know, but now Steve . . ."

"What happened to him?"

"The night of the storm he tripped over Winchester, fell down the stairs, and broke a tendon in his leg. It snapped just like a rubber band, the doctor said. He's got to stay off that leg for three weeks. It's one thing after another. First you getting hurt, and Jake, then Steve. I wake up in the middle of the night and I hear things. The light goes on by itself. I wouldn't mind if . . . if people weren't getting hurt."

"So, you think it's the house," Laurel whispered. In her mind arguments raged—tell him. No, don't you dare. Why not put his mind at rest? Be his friend? No. Great-grandfather wouldn't cause such harm, would he? Kindred spirit, he said—a living entity appearing to this boy, without a drop of Chinese blood in his body—how could Jonathan know Lin Peng?

Jonathan went on. "I remember how you told me I shouldn't sleep in that room. I told my uncle Jake about the—the thing. He's been hearing it too now.

87

The rattling in the morning. And then he told me about the golem."

Laurel stared at Jonathan. He was sweating; his face was flushed, and he kept picking at his fingers, as if he were trying to pick off glue. She asked him, "What's a golem?"

From the downstairs room came a long rattle and a final bam!, then silence.

"A ghost," said Jonathan. "Now, I know this sounds ridiculous, but listen. A golem, according to Jake, who has read about these things, is a special sort of ghost, made in Eastern Europe. It starts out small. And it . . . grows. It can become very strong. And destructive. Like, it can even kill a man, they say." Jonathan's voice rose as he swung his arms. "I know you'll think it's crazy," he said, "but I don't know. It fits."

"A—what kind of a ghost?"

"Well, actually," Jonathan picked his thumb, "a Jewish ghost. My mom thinks it's a poltergeist, but Jake says it sounds like a golem. I—I made it myself."

"Come on," said Laurel. She almost laughed.

"Not actually *him*—but I have this model and . . . it's hard to explain. It's like—I made the prototype, and things took off from there. The golem is like—well, it's like this model I made, part plastic, part clay. Certain words, incantations . . ."

"Did you make an incantation?" Laurel asked, fascinated.

"Not exactly. Except, I think I said something like, 'Go get him.' "

"So, who did this golem go for?"

"Well, I told you, it almost killed Steve."

"How could it do that?"

"There was a terrible crash. A huge crystal vase fell down in the pantry and broke into smithereens. That's what made Steve run down. He thought there was a burglar. Then he tripped on Winchester and fell down the stairs. He could have been killed. And it was my fault." Jonathan looked as if his eyes stung. In fact, he looked ready to cry.

Laurel asked him, "Why would this golem want to hurt Steve?"

Jonathan covered his mouth with his hand, and between his fingers came the muffled words, "Because I commanded it."

Steve hobbled in. "Hey! You ought to try that punching bag, Jonathan. It really feels good. Oh, excuse me. I didn't know you had a guest. Hi, Laurel."

"Hello, sir," said Laurel.

Steve's left leg was bound in tape, up to the knee. Under one arm he held a crutch. Behind him came Jake, on two crutches. His left hand was bandaged.

Jake smiled at Laurel. "Hi! Welcome to Splint City."

Laurel giggled in spite of herself.

"How're you doing?" Jake looked her over. "Um— you're fine, that cut's all healed. Jonathan said you were getting into the Youth Symphony—I'm impressed."

"I missed the tryout," Laurel told him. "Because of—" she sighed, "the accident."

"Oh, what a shame," said Jake, frowning in sympathy. "I guess I was so involved in my own problems that I didn't realize what this did to you." He eased himself down on the sofa, one leg extended. Suddenly he grinned at Laurel. "You wanna hear something terrific?"

She nodded.

Jake picked up the remote and the stereo went on—Boom! Boom! Tutadumdum. The room erupted in music, wailing and leaping and wild.

Laurel had never heard anything like it. It bounced and slid and climbed and dipped.

From upstairs came a series of yips and a long howl: Winchester singing along.

Jake picked up a tambourine and shook it to the beat, using his left hand. Steve tapped two pencils on the coffee table, creating a click-click percussion that seemed to fit. That was the amazing thing about this music: Whatever anyone added, it seemed to blend in and enhance the tune.

Laurel listened, her feet and fingers tingling. Suddenly she wanted more than anything to play her flute, play and play to this wild and wonderful music, let the notes find their own melodies, improvising, circling, climbing!

The garage door banged open, and Jonathan turned off the stereo. "Mom's home," he explained to Laurel. "Hates klezmer."

Laurel said, "I thought she worked for a record company."

"She hears music all day, she says," replied Jonathan. "At home she likes the silence."

"If once she'd listen to klezmer," Jake put in morosely, "she'd see. It's got soul. Not to say anything against your mother, Jonathan, but . . . she has strong opinions of her own."

Laurel looked from one to the other—extremists, all

of them, she thought, but funny and friendly. She liked them and wanted to stay.

"Want to see Winchester now?" Jonathan asked.

She nodded. They walked slowly up the stairs, where Winchester lay on top, guarding the staircase.

Laurel braced herself and inched her way forward. With her eyes closed, she let the dog sniff her leg. The wet tickle and the hot breath almost made her scream. But she said, "Hi, Winchester. Good dog."

"He likes you, Laurel," said Jonathan. He held the dog back by the collar, quickly bent down to stroke the wet muzzle with his fingertips, and whispered something into the dog's ear.

Winchester heaved over on one side, looking deflated. Everything about him sagged, from his jowls to his eyes and the flabby skin across his back.

"He looks sad," Laurel whispered. Something about the animal seemed very familiar—the broad, wrinkled head, the loose jowls, the sheer ugliness.

Laurel crept toward the dog. She crouched down beside him, then reached out and gingerly touched Winchester's massive, wrinkled head. It was the first time in her life that Laurel had ever willingly touched a dog.

Winchester's fur felt warm and slightly damp. "Good dog," Laurel whispered.

A floating feeling overwhelmed her. She had approached her "dragon"! Now the pearl. Now surely to reward her courage Great-grandfather would emerge from the spaces where his spirit lodged, from the eaves under the roofline, from the tree, tangled into its branches and leaves, from within the tinkling notes of the wind chimes. He would come to her, merge with her music. At the very moment of transformation she would run outside, and the ghost would follow.

"Excuse me a minute?" Laurel asked, implying she would use the bathroom.

"Sure," said Jonathan cheerfully, going on downstairs.

Laurel moved slowly. She mustn't appear too eager. Her backpack was still slung over her shoulder. She could put the flute together in an instant. Just two minutes on the window seat, playing her flute. . . .

Great-grandfather had obviously turned rambunctious, as ghosts sometimes do, striking out, causing commotion and damage. Mr. Wu had warned her of this. Even spirits can change. Maybe it was because he felt abandoned. Well, she would take him away. It would solve everybody's problems.

Laurel walked up the stairs. To her right was the room that had once been her father's study. The door was slightly ajar. Laurel looked in. A flowered cushion covered the window seat. But at the window there was a void. The oak tree was gone.

Stunned, Laurel seemed to fly down; she missed the last two stairs and landed on her hands and knees on the bottom, embarrassed, the wind knocked out of her.

"What happened to the tree?" she gasped, almost crying. "The tree!"

Jonathan rushed over. He reached out to help Laurel up off the floor.

"I had the gardener cut it down," said Steve. "It was a hazard. Are you okay? What's the matter with those damn *stairs*! This place is a real menace."

"You're telling me," said Jake, rubbing his wrist.

Laurel managed to catch her breath. "I'm okay," she said. "But the tree . . ."

"The gardener took it down this morning. Sawed it into firewood. It's all out there. Maybe your parents would like some wood," offered Steve.

Jonathan's mom came in. She wore a purple jumpsuit and long crystal earrings. "Hi, Laurel," she said cheerfully. "Have your dad call us if he wants some wood. It's a shame we had to cut that beautiful tree, but it was dangerous."

Laurel could hardly think. The tree! Gone! "What about the wind chimes?" she asked.

Jonathan reached into a shelf in the bookcase and held out three thin silvery slats. "This is all I could find. Do you want these?"

Laurel nodded, took the pieces, and slipped them into her backpack.

Now she knew. The spirit of the house—Great-grandfather—had somehow merged into that golem-thing. It was loose. It had become harmful, where once it was friendly. Maybe, like a mischievous child, it meant no real harm, didn't know its own strength. Still, a spirit on the loose could be dangerous.

She must call Mr. Wu and get him over here somehow. But why would this family agree to consult a fêng shui man? They'd think it was all nonsense.

Laurel drew herself up tall, lifted her head high, as her mother did when she was making a decision. "I want to tell you something," she said.

Laurel felt all their eyes upon her. She almost laughed; they were quite a crew, with their crutches and bandages and frowns.

"When we lived here, my mother put up a Chinese

mirror on the back wall in your room, Jonathan. It seems like—maybe—" Laurel stammered, "the house needs things like that. A mirror brings good luck."

"Ah," said Jake. "You think we can do something to improve our luck here?"

"It's worth a try," put in Steve.

"Keeping the house spirits happy," said Mom with a chuckle.

Laurel said, "We would be glad to give you one."

She calculated her savings; she had more than sixty dollars in the bank, birthday money from last year. It would be worth the sacrifice.

Steve laughed. "Sounds like we need it. The house spirits have been doing quite a number on us."

"How would we find the right thing?" asked Jonathan's mother.

"My mother and I will get it for you in Chinatown," said Laurel. "Chinese mirrors, you know, are different from regular mirrors. They are made of metal, not glass. You can't see yourself in them."

"They're not for fixing your hair," Jake put in, hobbling toward Laurel. "You use them to deflect evil spirits."

Jonathan's mom looked surprised. "How do you know these things, Jake?"

"Oh, just poking around old books," said Jake with a slight smile.

He stood leaning on his crutches. "If you could pick it out," he said, "I'll buy it for them as a house-warming present. What does such a thing cost?"

"Maybe thirty dollars," said Laurel, greatly relieved.

"It's a deal," said Jake. He took three ten-dollar

bills from his pocket and gave them to Laurel, shaking her hand as he did. It was warm and sweaty and fleshy.

"That's very kind of you, Laurel," said Jonathan's mom. "And you too, Jake. Now, Steve and I have to go fix dinner," she said, and they went out to the kitchen.

Laurel was amazed. Her father never cooked, never even entered the kitchen. Nor would her mom have approved.

Laurel turned to Jake. "That music you played before," she began, "is it hard to learn?"

"Not really," said Jake. "I have some of the scores written down. Then, of course, when we all get together, we improvise."

"Like jazz," said Laurel. "I've never really played jazz."

"You should try klezmer. We could use a flute. Flute is so expressive, beautiful, and what range! Did you like my music? Didn't it make you want to play?"

Laurel laughed; the man was so exuberant, even on crutches! "Yes," she said. "It did."

Jake seemed about to say more, but suddenly Winchester came up behind him and nearly knocked him over. Head down, Winchester pushed his way between Jake and Laurel and heaved his massive body out the door.

Jonathan rushed out after him. "Winchester! Winchester! Come back here."

Laurel followed, with a wave to Jake.

Jonathan called the dog again and again. At last he turned to Laurel with a shrug. "Doesn't mind. Not at all."

"I thought you were going to get a puppy," said Laurel. "Isn't it easier to train a puppy?" She chuckled. "Look. He's making a hole."

They watched as Winchester rooted around a tree, rather like a pig looking for truffles.

"He's a weird dog," Jonathan said.

"Don't you like him?"

"At first I didn't," Jonathan said. He twisted his mouth and squirmed. "I just got him because—well, I had reasons. Now, you know, he's not bad. He kind of grows on you."

"Before," said Laurel, "I saw you talking to him."

Jonathan bit his lips, then he smiled. "Yeah, well," he said, "Winchester's okay." He changed the subject. "Have you started your Human Heritage report yet?"

"Oh, you have to do that one too?"

"All the seventh-grade social studies classes have it. What are you going to do?"

"I haven't decided," Laurel said. Social studies was the last thing on her mind these days, but time was closing in on her again; the report was due in less than two weeks and had to be based on her personal heritage.

They walked a little ways. Swaying from side to side like an ailing man, Winchester followed.

"Why did you want the golem to get rid of Steve?" Laurel asked. "He seems—well, he seems nice."

Jonathan shrugged. "Why don't you want your grandparents to live with you?"

"Who said I don't?"

"It's obvious," Jonathan said. "Whenever anyone mentions them, you get that strange look on your face. You clam up."

"And you don't like Steve," Laurel said. She wished she hadn't begun this conversation. She certainly had no intention of discussing her personal feelings with anybody, least of all this boy who thought he had built a ghost.

"It's not that I don't like him," Jonathan began. "I mean, he thinks he's so hot. Always jogging and rowing and batting that ball. He's too much. He signed me up for this ten-K race without even asking me. Just to get an old sweatshirt."

"Lots of kids are running in that race," Laurel said. "Are you?"

"No. I'm not good at sports."

"Well, you don't have to be," said Jonathan. "You're such a great flute player. I bet you'll be in the high school marching band and everything."

"Why should . . ."

But they were interrupted by coughing, hacking, and wheezing. Winchester seemed to be in agony. The dog squeezed himself together like an accordion, then lengthened like a python as he let out a last lingering cough.

"What's wrong with him?" Laurel ran up to the dog. Winchester retched, brought up a small stream of yellow liquid, then sank down on the lawn, exhausted.

Jonathan rushed down beside Winchester, cradling the dog's head in his lap. "Winchester, what's wrong?" He bent close to Winchester and kissed his head.

Laurel had never seen anyone kiss a dog. It made her feel odd, sort of soft and squishy inside, almost like crying.

97

"Is Winchester sick?" Laurel asked. "Does he need a vet?"

Jonathan shook his head. "I'm not sure. Sometimes dogs eat grass and throw up. He's done this before. I guess he'll be okay."

She said, "He almost looks like a dragon. A Chinese dragon."

Jonathan stood up. "That's what the tree said. Something about a dragon. Slaying a dragon."

Laurel thought of her fortune. "He who fears the dragon cannot capture the pearl." It was true—things appear as people need them, whether in a fortune cookie or as a voice on the wind. Could it be that Jonathan had a dragon in his life too?

She glanced at the boy; of course he did. People are all alike. She had always been told this. It never seemed more clear than now.

"You could do a report about dragons," Jonathan suggested. "I'll bet there's tons of information about that."

Laurel shrugged. "What are you going to do?"

"I guess I'll find out more about this golem for my report. Kill two birds with one stone."

"I guess I will do dragons," Laurel decided. She softened. "Want to go to the library together? We'd have to carpool. The big library is over in San Rafael."

"Sure," said Jonathan. "Only, neither Steve nor Jake can drive now, so unless my mom can get off on Saturday . . ."

"Saturdays are out," said Laurel. "I have Chinese school."

"Oh! What's it like?"

"It's okay. The kids get kind of rowdy. Sometimes they're a pain. See, they all live in the city. I'm the only one from Marin. They have this little clique going. . . ."

Jonathan nodded. "Sounds like Hebrew school. I'm supposed to go, but I told them, no way."

"So, how will you learn it?"

"Oh, I already know Hebrew. It's the other stuff, special prayers, and also you're supposed to be part of the—well, they call it the 'community.' You know."

Laurel shook her head. "Not exactly. We have . . ." She took a deep breath. She had never really liked explaining things to the kids in school; it felt like she was a representative of a whole people, instead of just being herself. With Jonathan, however, it seemed okay. "We have big families. I mean, really huge clans. In all of China there are only about one hundred surnames and billions of people. I'm a Wang, so anybody who is a Wang has a special relationship with other Wangs—that's our community."

"And you learn to speak Chinese for your religion?"

Laurel laughed. "No. I'm a Methodist. We learn it so we can talk to our ancestors." Having said this, she felt herself flush.

But Jonathan didn't seem to think it odd. He only nodded, as if he understood perfectly.

9

*

Laurel and her mother drove across the bridge to the city.

"I have to make a report about my heritage," Laurel told her. "For school. I'm going to write about the dragon."

"Why, Laurel, that's a great idea." Her mother smiled. "I'm a dragon, you know. This is what gives me my high energy."

"I know," said Laurel. "Do you believe in these signs?"

Her mother smiled. "I like being a dragon," she said, ignoring the question. "And you? Monkey?"

"The monkey is called lazy," Laurel said gloomily.

"Only if you look at the negative. Monkey is clever. Monkey is inquisitive and very loving." Mom glanced at her watch. "We have time, I think, to stop and buy that mirror for your friends before school. You see, they are not Chinese, but they appreciate the grace and beauty of Chinese things."

Laurel kept her mouth shut.

"I also have to stop at Macy's," Mom said with sudden briskness. "I need to buy some more sheets for your grandparents' beds. And small bowls. My father hates eating from large plates. He always thought it was indelicate. And I want to buy some pretty artificial flowers, something that won't look cheap—there must be decent ones around."

Laurel heard the anxiety in her mother's voice.

"Ma," she said, using the Chinese word. "How long is it since you have seen your parents?"

Her mother's face remained set, but Laurel could discern a slight change, like a shadow. "I was eleven when I last saw them," she said. "Just a little younger than you are now."

"But still you know what your father likes?" Laurel said. "How do you know he has not changed?"

"Of course I know," her mother said sharply. "How could I forget? Older people don't—they don't change. We have kept in touch, after all."

Laurel thought of the letters that came every month, the words formal and restrained. "Dear daughter, we hope you are well. We send greetings to your husband and child; we thank you for the photographs in your last letter. I send you here a picture of your father and me, taken in a small restaurant by the park."

Photographs were all alike, flat and solemn, even if the people were smiling. The smiles were only external, like decorations pasted on. One could not tell at all what lay behind them.

Laurel's mother parked the car in a garage on Mason Street. They walked over to Chinatown, bustling past the many shops until Mom found the very one she wanted. Inside, the courtesies began, Mom chattering in Mandarin, nodding, smiling, nodding again as she bargained. To buy for the first stated price was considered stupid and discourteous; the shopkeeper wanted to achieve a just sale.

101

At last they selected a heavy, round bronze mirror with a fine embossed dragon, its talons upraised and holding a spray of budding flowers. They waited while the shopkeeper wrapped it in heavy red paper, tied with a golden ribbon.

"After this we better hurry," Laurel's mother said. "You can walk over to the school by yourself while I get the car and go straight to Macy's. Two hours is hardly enough—why are we always running out of time?"

Laurel watched her mom walk quickly out of Chinatown. She was so pretty, so energetic! It was true, she had the passion of a dragon. She seemed to breathe fire when she was angry. She was shrewd and healthy and very lucky.

"Lucky for me," Laurel's mom had said a thousand times, then quoted some incident. Or did she have a way of making her own luck?

Laurel headed up the hill toward the tall, narrow building that stood on the incline, attached as most San Francisco houses are. Mrs. Chen's building was painted a dull yellow, the color almost worn to ash. The wooden windowsills and doors were rough and splintered. A grocery store occupied the bottom story; above it were apartments, the middle apartment belonging to Mrs. Chen. She had converted her living room into a schoolroom, making of one entire wall a chalkboard and filling the room with chairs and old wooden tables left from some school or office, long retired. In the tiny kitchen Mrs. Chen sometimes made tea for her students, if it was a special occasion and the children were good. She served tea on a beautiful blue-and-white tray, laden with sesame cookies and salted almonds.

Laurel walked up the narrow stairs. The carpet was gray-green, worn and matted. The walls of the place always seemed damp and buckling with age.

Laurel checked her watch. She was still a little early. She might have browsed for a few minutes in the stores, looking at jewelry and embroidered jackets. Now she would be forced to spend time alone with Mrs. Chen, watching that delicate fluttering of eyelids and hands, hearing that birdlike voice talking about silly, inconsequential things.

But when Laurel rang the bell, there was no gentle voice, only a cry in anguished and rapid Chinese, followed in English. "Oh! It's terrible. Terrible. What can I do? The police said to leave it. They are coming. The police! The police!"

Laurel peered inside at the schoolroom. Across the green chalkboard someone had painted, in thick red letters, YELLOW DEVILS! GO BACK TO CHINK-LAND.

She felt a tightening in her chest, a throbbing in her ears. Yellow devils! She had heard of times, far in the past, when racists screamed slogans at the poor Chinese laborers. Hoodlums, they caught the men and cut off their pigtails, jeered at the women, subjected them to humiliations. It had all seemed unbelievable. Now, here before her, the walls seemed to drip with blood. Someone had smeared them with red paint. And Mrs. Chen, wide-eyed and pale, stood trembling, trying to be brave.

A moment later Laurel heard sirens. Two policemen came running up the stairs. "Mrs. Chen? Come outside with us, please. We got here as soon as we could—we just got a call at the station. Now, this is probably just a scare, but we have to evacuate the building. Someone said they planted a bomb."

"Where? Where?" Mrs. Chen clasped her hands under her throat.

"Here. In your apartment. We have to get everyone out of here quick."

Jonathan, Steve, Jake, and Mom sat in the kitchen. It was Monday. Blue Monday, his mother said.

"I should have known it," said Jonathan's mom. "Bad luck comes in threes."

"Now, Marion," said Steve, rubbing her back, "don't tell me you're superstitious."

"It's this house," she said flatly. "Ever since we moved here, everything's gone wrong." She sniffed, blew her nose, muffling her words, "We were so happy before."

"Sweetheart, be reasonable," said Steve. "This has nothing to do with the house. There's one thing I know. Your company has been on the skids for a long time. You knew they were on the verge of bankruptcy. Look, maybe this is a blessing in disguise."

"It's pretty darn well-disguised!" Mom wept. "One more week, and I'm out of there. Where am I going to find another job?"

Mom had made a huge bowl of popcorn, her remedy for a crisis. An enormous cavity in the middle of the bowl showed what they had already consumed, the four of them, munching and worrying.

"Steve's right," said Jake, his mouth full of popcorn. "This could all turn out for the best."

Jonathan ate another handful of popcorn. He took a

swallow of 7UP. He wished he could tell them—it was his fault.

Jake had gone out into the backyard. He lay on the lounge, reading, his crutches propped beside him.

Mom and Steve were in the workout room. But Jonathan heard none of the sounds of equipment, no punching, grinding, or clattering. He had walked past and heard them talking, their voices sharp, coming in rapid bursts.

Fighting, Jonathan thought. Good. Maybe she'd tell Steve to get lost. Jake would stay here in the house. He'd move into the den. Everything would be terrific. Jonathan would have his own space again. He'd have his uncle here. He'd be rid of Steve. Terrific.

Jonathan sat down at his worktable. All his models stood in a row, plus the box for a new one called Argos the Magnificent Athlete. Argos had joints that moved. He came equipped with a bicycle with pedals and wheels that actually turned. Steve had brought the model to Jonathan from Palm Springs many months ago. Jonathan had laid it aside. He wouldn't accept the gift. No way.

Now, curiosity and desire and another feeling that he couldn't quite name made Jonathan pick up the box and open it. He spread the parts out on the table. Inside, added to the directions, was a paragraph about athletes, how they have to train, and some of the feats achieved by the greats.

This wasn't a bad model, Jonathan thought to himself with a smile. Actually it was pretty neat.

He began to assemble the body. It was his usual

method; body comes first, then limbs, then head, then all the extras.

But words intruded. Shouts.

First his mother. Then Steve. He had never heard them fighting before. It was fascinating. It was frightening.

"So why didn't you ever tell me . . . ?" His mother's voice was high, tense, and shrill.

"What difference did it make? I didn't care. I thought it was what you wanted, Marion."

"So you just went ahead and let me be a phony!"

"Why is it my fault if you keep on pretending to be something you're not. How should I know you hated your job and the gym and everything else . . . ?"

"I didn't know what else do to! Do you know what it's like being left alone with a kid to support? And no insurance. Nothing! It changes you. Oh, boy, it sure does."

Jonathan felt sick inside. He wanted to shut his door and turn on his Walkman and drown out their voices.

Instead he opened his door wider.

"I hate those creeps!" his mother shouted, her voice heavy now with tears and with rage. "I had to try to fit in, don't you see? They were all so—so jazzed up, funky. Okay, if that's what it took, I could do it too! I got so sick of hearing about Karma and *kuṇḍalinī* from those phonies I thought I'd puke!"

"What's that got to do with me? You're saying I forced you to do all these things. You hate jogging, you hate bicycling. . . ."

"I don't hate it! I don't love it either. I had to do something, can't you see that? I was lonely. Where would I ever meet anyone? So I joined the stupid gym, started eating tofu and sunflower seeds and yogurt—I'd give my soul for a New York corned beef sandwich!"

"Baby, baby . . ." Steve tried to calm her, but she was raging, pounding on something, probably the punching bag, for the sounds came through the walls, thuds and rattles, in rhythm with her fury.

"They had *promised* me I could make *records*. What'd I do? I had to *sit* there and give people the *ax*, month after month after *month*. . . . I never had the guts to leave. I'm a coward. *A total coward*." Bam! Bam! Bam!

"So, change it."

"I can't. They already fired me! I can't quit."

"No, but you can start. Baby, baby, listen to me. There's one thing I know. You're an artistic person. A creative person. Get into music. Take a chance. I'll change this room into a studio. I'll get soundproofing. We'll buy the machines you need. I can get a loan on the car. . . ."

"You'd do that? For me?"

It was silent then. Jonathan felt his face burning. His chest ached, as if something were broken within.

He picked up piece after piece of Argos the Magnificent Athlete. Then he laid his head down on his worktable and wished he could cry. But for years and years, ever since he became the man of the house, Jonathan had never allowed himself that.

In the night Jonathan suddenly awoke. The room was silent. That was odd. No snores issued from Uncle Jake, and none came from the top of the stairs where Winchester slept.

Jonathan sat up. There by the window stood Uncle Jake, outlined against the windowpane, a large, bulky shape.

"What's wrong, Uncle Jake?" whispered Jonathan.

Jake scratched his head, turning toward Jonathan. "I thought you said the wind chimes were broken."

"They are. I gave the pieces to Laurel."

"Then how could the darn things wake me up?" Jake demanded. He strode across the room, snapped on the small lamp by his bed. In the shadows his face looked gloomy, puffy. "I heard them," he said.

Jonathan got up. He went to the window and peered out. "Do you believe in ghosts?" he asked.

Uncle Jake sighed. "Well, let's get some definition," he said. "What exactly is a ghost? A spirit? The Unseen? Of course I believe in those. You know," he added, "we should study together again. It was good when we did."

"Yes," Jonathan admitted. "It was."

Jake got up and began to pace, his crutches thudding on the floor. "It's all my fault," he said morosely. He swung himself down again onto Jonathan's bed.

"What's your fault?"

"Your mom losing her job. The tension in the house. Everything."

"How could it be your fault?" Jonathan demanded, amazed that Jake should take this upon himself.

"Well, your mother's been pretty tense with me around. Aggravated. Trying to conceal it. So she probably let it out on the people at work. And they fired her. Besides, it's what I've always wanted."

"What? You wanted her to get fired?"

"I wanted her to get away from that outfit she's

108

with, yes. Because they produce nothing but junk, and they won't let your mother use her talent. She's one of the best recording engineers I know, and they just use her in the front office. It makes me sick!"

"Why don't you tell her?" Jonathan exclaimed.

"I'm going to leave tomorrow," said Jake.

"No!" cried Jonathan. He glanced around the room, trying to imagine how spacious it would be without Jake's clutter.

"After next week your mom will be home more. The two of us would just get on each other's nerves. It wouldn't be fair to you and Steve." He shrugged. "I don't mean to bug her. We're just too much alike."

"Too alike?" said Jonathan. "I always thought you were too different. That's what my mother says."

"Tut-tut-tut, I wouldn't want to contradict your mother," said Jake, wiping his brow. "But, you see . . . we are on opposite sides of the same coin. I like old. She likes new. I like klezmer. She likes reggae. She eats healthy, I eat junk. We're both messy, but in different ways. Your mother cultivates plants; I cultivate books. Both of us don't know when to quit. Besides, it's time for me to get back to my cronies. I can't stay here forever."

"But, Jake, you can't get around."

"I'll manage."

"But, Jake, can't you wait a few days? We haven't done any of the things we planned. We were going to go hiking and rummaging through the bookstores and the library, we were going to study together, we were going to make music. . . ."

"I'm a little slowed down right now," said Jake, lifting his wrist, smiling sadly. "Another time. I would have loved to go to that big library you were talking about."

"Laurel's dad is taking us tomorrow after school. Why don't you wait and come with us?"

"I hear they have a wonderful music collection," said Uncle Jake, his tone wistful. "I guess one more day . . ."

"Won't hurt," Jonathan finished for him.

He felt guilty and mean; he didn't want Jake to leave, but he didn't exactly want him to stay either. He wondered, When would he ever get his feelings straightened out?

In the night Winchester started to sniffle and snuffle and cough. Jonathan heard him from the hallway. Then the dog would groan.

Jonathan got up to give him water. Jonathan patted his side. The dog's chest heaved in and out like a bellows.

Jonathan laid his head down gently upon the dog's side, to hear its breathing. It seemed very odd to realize that this animal had a heart and lungs and maybe even a soul. A definite personality.

"Don't be sick, Winchester," Jonathan whispered. He laid down on the carpet beside his dog and fell asleep.

Ten more days. It was a countdown. Grandmother and Grandfather would arrive.

Laurel was seized with restlessness, especially now, after what had happened at Chinese school. What to do? Where to go? How to feel?

She had been terrified, of course. Then anger set in.

Now that burning fear and anger came over Laurel again. She remembered the humiliation of standing there on the street with the sirens screaming, as if *she* were a criminal, someone to be stared at and pointed at and talked about.

Those two hours had been the longest of Laurel's life. Over and over she asked herself, How could anyone do such a thing to gentle, delicate Mrs. Chen? How dare they break into her home and smear her walls and call her names? And why?

When Laurel's mother came to get her, the street was blocked off with police cars and two fire trucks, their red lights flashing, and officers rushing about, searching from the cellars to the rooftops. For an entire block all buildings were evacuated. A large crowd choked the streets.

Laurel heard her mother calling long before she could get to her. "Laurel! Laurel!" She screamed, both in Mandarin and English, the agony in her voice more profound than any words. "My child! My girl-child— who has seen her? My child!" And when at last she saw Laurel, she burst into weeping, rushed to pull Laurel close to her and tight, so tight, that Laurel could hardly breathe, and her mother's tears covered Laurel's face and neck.

"Ma! Ma!" Laurel wept. "I'm all right. I'm fine. Look, I'm fine."

Later when Laurel and her parents sat together by the fire drinking hot cinnamon tea, and her mother had very nearly composed herself, they talked. Laurel had heard the story before, of course, but never this way, all at once and complete, as if her mom were living it again.

Her mother's voice was heavy, like the dusk, filled with broken sobs and pauses when the memories were too sharp.

"It was the same way. In China. Suddenly everything changed. Sirens. Soldiers on the street. Threats against the intellectuals, the upper classes. My father was a professor. My mother, a businesswoman. Successful. We thought—it seemed reasonable—ha! Under tyrants, is there any reason?"

"Shh—Jacqueline, it was long ago, my dear. It was so terrible, how you suffered. Try to forget."

"Such things are never forgotten, Frank. I try to forget, not ever to speak about it. But Laurel must know this. It is her heritage too." Laurel's mother took a sip of tea, a deep breath, then continued.

"My parents and I had traveled to Hong Kong. There was a conference. My ma so loved the shopping there in Hong Kong—we were to be gone for ten days. But Ma was called back home. Emergency in one of her buildings. A woman of great character, she knew her responsibility. So she went back. It was decided I would stay with my father, to enjoy the vacation.

"But then—then! Oh, God, they closed China. Closed the country. It was horrible. Nobody could get out. Nobody could go in. We heard about beatings, arrests, torture. How could we get in again to join my ma? And if we went home, would we be safe? Could we ever leave again?" Her face seemed to freeze into a mask of fury. "Cultural revolution." She spat the words. "Devils! What revolution? What culture? They were just hoodlums, like all criminals, wanting to be boss."

Her mother's face was taut, her eyes snapping fire. Laurel had sat, speechless, numb, her hands clenched, listening to this tale. She could almost imagine her mother at eleven, small and terrified. She wished she could say something tender and kind and helpful. But she could only listen and stare.

"So my father made arrangements to send me away—out of the country. He was afraid that as he attempted to get back into China he might be arrested. He did not want to have me with him. They did—they did things. Even to children. So he arranged with my auntie in Santa Barbara. And he sent me alone on the airplane. I never really said good-bye to my ma. I never knew I would not see her again for so many, many years."

Now the new sheets were on the beds in the extra room, the room Laurel's mom had spent weeks fixing. The floor was a deeply shaded, highly polished wood with a brand new woven rug. The chairs, the little table, the cupboard—all were polished and sweet smelling, and the bedspreads bore large red peonies and dark green leaves on a white background. The curtains were crisp and white, delicate as butterflies' wings.

Laurel stood in the room. Soon, so soon, she thought, with that heavy, clutching feeling inside. On the new bureau stood a beautiful statue of a pair of birds, phoenixes, for luck, and a porcelain vase with three artificial roses in it. Everything was perfect for her mother's parents. And now, for the first time, Laurel trembled, not for herself, but for her mom.

How must her mother feel, after all these years, to be seeing her parents again? Scared. Timid. Excited. She must be thinking over and over, Will they like me? Will they like my husband and my child? Are they angry that I abandoned them? Yes, yes, they told me to go and live with Auntie. But maybe a better daughter, a more respectful child, would have insisted upon staying with her parents. She would have wanted to be there to care for them in their old age. Now all these many years have passed. What can we say to one another? How can we ever catch up?

Laurel went into the living room. She stood by the table where the dragons guarded the picture of Great-grandfather. Beneath the portrait stood a small incense burner and a packet of incense sticks ready for use.

"Laurel! Laurel!" her father called. "Come on. I'm ready now. Let's go to the library."

"Are you going to drop us off?"

"No, I think I'll go in too. I want to look at some architectural magazines."

"You are hovering over me, Dad," said Laurel, but she said it with a smile. Her parents were being superprotective. In fact, they had both agreed that she no longer had to go to Chinese school if she didn't want to. Her luck, it seemed, was changing.

10

*

They walked up the path to the house. "Jonathan's mom lost her job," said Laurel. "More bad luck."

"You're a good friend, Laurel," said her father. He nodded at the package Laurel was carrying, wrapped in red paper.

Jonathan answered the door.

Steve called out, "Come in! Come in! Have a seat."

They sat down opposite Jake, who rose from the sofa and nodded a greeting, then sat back down, smiling. "Yiddish," he said, pointing to the stereo.

From the stereo came music, soulful and yearning. A woman sang in words that Laurel could not understand, but somehow the meanings were clear. It was a song of sorrow, loss, eventual forgiveness, and hope.

It was completely different in beat and style from the klezmer music Laurel had heard here last time, but Laurel could tell it was the same sort of music. She felt entranced.

"That's wonderful," said Laurel's father when the song ended.

Laurel gave Jake the package. He presented it to Steve.

"May I open it?" Steve asked. He looked flustered

and almost shy, as if he had hardly ever received a gift in his life.

"Sure," said Jake with a flourish. "Be my guest."

Steve ripped open the paper, pulled out the brass mirror, and held it up admiringly. "Wow! Thanks," he said. "Thank you, Jake, and you, Laurel, for getting it. Now, I guess we're set for life."

"I guess it depends on what you believe," said Laurel's dad. "What brings luck?" he posed the question earnestly, leaning forward in his chair. "The method or the man?"

"That sounds very Jungian," said Jake.

"It is," said Laurel's dad. "Are you interested in Jung?"

"Why, very much so," said Jake excitedly. "I've read about his idea of collective unconscious."

"I hear you are coming with us to the library. We will have a lot to talk about. Right now, I'm not sure I believe in luck. You see, we just had the fêng shui man at our house. . . ."

"Fêng shui?" asked Steve.

"The idea that changing the environment can improve your luck. The art of placing things."

Jake nodded. "I've heard about that," he said.

Laurel got a strange, sinking feeling. She did not want her father to say anything more. But he did.

"So you can imagine how upsetting it was," he said, "the very week after we had the fêng shui scholar, a terrible thing happened to Laurel."

"What happened?" everyone asked.

Laurel glanced at Jonathan. Their eyes met. Laurel knew Jonathan was thinking the same thing as she— the ghost. Or was it the golem?

"There was a bomb scare at her Chinese school. Poor Laurel had to wait out on the street with her teacher for more than two hours. The other children, of course, just walked home. It was very frightening. . . . The police searched the entire building several times. They did find a device."

"A bomb?" asked Steve.

"No. But something resembling a bomb. And there were hate slogans painted on the walls. It's a horrible thing. A helpless feeling. Because these people are cowards. They won't show themselves, but only terrorize people. And they have no cause, except for hatred."

Jake nodded. "We know. It has happened to our people many, many times."

There was a silence, a collective sigh.

"What are you going to do?" asked Steve.

"What can we do?" said Laurel's dad. "It's up to Laurel. We won't make her go back to Chinese school. In fact, her mother now prefers that she doesn't go. It is strange. I was the one who thought it didn't really matter. After all, we are American. My family has been here for four generations. Laurel was born in Fresno, California. But after those hoodlums did this thing. . . ." He glanced at his watch. "We should be leaving. Do you want to come along, Steve?"

"No, thanks. I'm going to stick around and try to fix some supper. Marion's working late tonight. She said something about using the studio after hours."

Jake and Laurel's father talked all the way to the library, while Laurel and Jonathan sat in the backseat.

"How's Winchester?" Laurel asked.

"He's kind of listless," said Jonathan.

"Is he eating?" asked Laurel.

"Not much," said Jonathan.

"He could be sick," said Laurel.

"You know a lot about dogs, it sounds like," said Jonathan.

"I don't know anything about dogs," said Laurel.

"But you—you said you loved dogs. You said . . ."

"I lied," said Laurel. She stared straight ahead. Streaks of sunlight slipped past her vision, like darts. "I'm sorry."

"Why would you lie about liking dogs?" Jonathan exclaimed.

"Shh! You don't have to tell the whole world!" Laurel said.

But the men were talking so animatedly, they didn't even pause or turn.

"I wanted to get into the house," Laurel said. "I knew about the—you see, I've always—that is, it's not you, Jonathan. You didn't make a golem. It's me. Mine. The ghost, I mean."

Jake was talking with his hands now, laughing, leaning toward Laurel's father. And her father was nodding, beaming, emphasizing his points with his fist on the steering wheel.

"You knew about the ghost all the time?" Jonathan asked.

Laurel nodded. "I was trying to get it out for you. With my flute. But then you had the tree cut down."

"But what did the tree have to do with it?"

"It lived there," Laurel whispered. She closed her eyes. Surely Jonathan would think she was deranged.

"Here we are!" said her father brightly.

They all got out. Jake headed for the music section. Laurel's father went over to the fine arts collection. She and Jonathan stood by the reference desk.

"In the tree," Jonathan whispered. He nodded to himself.

"You don't think it's crazy?"

"Sure, it's crazy," he said, grinning. "But that doesn't mean I don't believe you. I told you the tree was talking."

"Is it possible," Laurel asked now, "for two people to share the . . . the same . . ."

"Hallucinations?" Jonathan finished the sentence for her. He scratched his head. "Maybe it is. Or maybe that mirror you brought us will get rid of it. I don't know. I'm going to try to find out about this golem thing."

"Well, I'll go do some research on dragons."

"There you go, Dragon Girl," Jonathan said with a grin.

"I'm not a dragon," Laurel said, unable to repress a smile. "I'm just a monkey."

"Dragon," said Jonathan. And she could tell he meant it as a compliment.

Golem, golem, golem. Jonathan studied the computer index. He glanced up. Behind the desk sat a librarian wearing a bulky green knit dress. She was a large woman, with reddish hair done in a strange, old-fashioned way. She got up. Jonathan saw that she wore black, thick-soled walking shoes, almost like a man. It was odd. Still she moved with a light step, a certain determined cheerfulness, coming toward him.

"Maybe I can help you?" she asked. "I'm Freda

Wczekowski, the research librarian." She chuckled softly. "Don't try to pronounce it. Everyone just calls me Freda."

"I'm looking for—ghosts," murmured Jonathan.

"Any special ghost? Is there something specific you want to know?"

Jonathan felt all clutched up. He felt absurd. How could he possibly say it? *I want to know how to kill a golem.*

Freda would naturally ask him: "What in the world are you talking about? First you imply that you have created such a thing, and next you tell me you want to kill it. Are you crazy?"

Jonathan glanced at the librarian. She seemed younger than he had first thought. Her hair glinted in the light, shimmering with streaks of bronze and gold. She had a nice smile.

"I want to research a golem," Jonathan said. "A Jewish ghost, for my school Human Heritage project."

"Well, yes, I'd begin with the *Jewish Encyclopedia,* over there," Freda said, taking brisk steps to the shelf, pulling out a volume, smacking it down smartly on the table. "And here—you might want to check this one, *Myths, Legends and Culture,* and this book about Eastern European traditions."

Jonathan was amazed at the growing stack of books around him, and he began to read first one item, then another. "The golem, according to tradition, can be created only by a highly devout and spiritually elevated person. There is a formula for the creation of the golem, handed down by Rabbi Lowe of Prague, who said he took clay from the riverbed and formed a creature, then, using mystical letters and Hebrew incantations, caused the breath of life to be . . ."

Jonathan read on and on and on. There were many legends of holy men in the Middle Ages, using meditation and holy names and numbers to breathe life into a man of earth and clay. Some even recorded the formula, although they warned people not to try it, for there was always the danger that the golem would turn on its creator. "Only the most pure, and the most pious, should dare to undertake this magic of creation, using the holy names." It all had to do with intention. "The golem is neither good nor evil," Jonathan read. "It is a matter of the intention of its creator. In some legends the golem saves an entire town of Jews from murdering bands. In another the golem itself destroys the town. One can learn from this theme that hatred becomes its own monster. An evil intention, like its manifestation, the golem, grows and grows, feeding upon itself, until it destroys everything in its path."

Jonathan stared at the page until the words became blurred before his eyes. He felt sick with guilt and shame. The evil intention was certainly his. He had even voiced it, *Go for it! Get rid of Steve.* And even if he had no real power to create a golem, still the words themselves were a destructive force. Somehow Jonathan knew that. He felt it in his bones.

Sure enough, the next book, dealing with *Creation, Legend and Psychology* told the following: "In Jewish tradition the word is the father of the deed. Vows and curses are never taken lightly. Our ancestors knew the power of words to harm or to inspire; they realized that, psychologically, actions follow words; to verbal-

ize an intention is almost as powerful as actually ful-
filling it."

"I have done an evil thing," Jonathan said, half
aloud.

He looked around for Jake. Jake was nowhere to be
seen. Jake would know some answers; in the old days
when they used to study together, Jake would pull
down the thick volumes one after the other, flip open
the heavy pages, run his finger down a column, and
exclaim, "Ah! Here—it says here . . ." and he would
expound a principle of the religious law, Talmud.

Jonathan, at six, seven, eight, and nine years of age,
would ask Jake, until it became sort of a joke between
them, "What are we studying today, Jake?"

Jake's answer was always the same: "Truth."

Once Jake had told him about the Hebrew word
emet, meaning truth. He wrote three Hebrew letters.
"Look at this—the word truth is spelled like this. Take
away the first letter, the *aleph*, and you have the word
death. Now, *aleph* is a silent letter. There are many
lessons in this. Often, to hear the truth, we must be silent. To speak hastily can mean death."

Jonathan shuddered. How come he remembered
these conversations from years ago? He felt burdened
with remembering. It would be better, far better, to
forget.

Overcome with sleepiness, Jonathan put his head
down on the table.

The next thing he knew, he heard voices from behind him. He listened. ". . . some fascinating papers
that were left by my uncle in the basement—I've
translated many of the letters. . . ."

"How exciting to find someone who cares about

these things! Ever since I was a little girl, I have loved history. . . ."

Jonathan turned. There, in an alcove by a window stood Jake, resting comfortably on his crutches, and Freda, the librarian. So immersed were they in conversation that when Mr. Wang came to get them and take them all home, Jake muttered and coughed and patted his pockets and blushed like a schoolboy—a boy in love.

All the way home Jake talked about Freda. "Brilliant woman. Mathematics background. Family from Lithuania and Poland—she understands history, let me tell you. She rolls those references off her fingertips— she's going to send for a journal for me from Albany, New York. Can you imagine? A person of real initiative."

"Nice looking too," said Mr. Wang.

Laurel and Jonathan laughed.

Jake patted his pockets and sat there grinning. Then soberly he said, "I never thought I would meet a woman like her. I had given up."

"Oh, one must never give up," said Mr. Wang heartily. "Especially where romance is concerned."

Laurel and Jonathan grinned at each other, and Jonathan felt his heart racing. Uncle Jake in love! Could it happen so quickly? Maybe not for everyone, but Uncle Jake was unique. All his decisions were sudden and quick—like finding an apartment, starting a band, deciding upon a car, and now, finally, maybe, a wife.

Home, the house looked oddly quiet and cold. Jonathan fumbled with his key. Jake rang the bell. Nobody came.

"Why wouldn't Steve leave the porch light on for us?" Jake wondered.

"Looks like maybe he left in a hurry." Jonathan was gripped with foreboding. Maybe there had been another accident. A sudden illness. His mom. Or Steve. He could hardly speak; his teeth were chattering. "Do you . . . think something happened?"

"I don't know," said Jake.

At last the key worked. The door sprang open.

Jonathan snapped on all the lights. "Mom! Steve! Are you guys home?"

He ran into the kitchen to look for a note, back to the living room, where Jake stood looking around, rubbing the back of his neck. "Where's the dog?" he asked.

Then Jonathan realized it. Winchester was gone too.

11

*

Steve, Mom, Jake, and Jonathan sat in the kitchen. Jonathan had sent out for delicatessen. The kitchen seemed to drip garlic and spices; the smell was heavenly.

"I don't know how you did it," said Jake, taking a big bite of his corned beef and coleslaw sandwich.

"You do what you have to do," said Mom with a misty look at Steve.

"It was nothing," Steve said modestly.

"You carried him? Carried him to the car?" Jonathan couldn't help repeating it. It was hard to believe that anyone could carry Winchester, least of all someone with a broken tendon, needing a crutch.

"I had no choice," said Steve. "The dog was— well, he was gagging and retching terribly. He even brought up some blood. I thought—I was so scared he'd die. I knew I had to get him to the vet fast."

"It's amazing," said Jake, "the strength you find, when you're in a crisis. Some people have been known to lift up cars."

"How did you know where the vet was?" asked Jonathan's mom.

"I had made a mental note of it," Steve said. "There's one thing I know. It pays to be prepared."

"It sure does," said Jonathan. He felt very odd. Weepy.

"When will they know?" he asked Steve, for perhaps the tenth time.

Steve glanced at his watch. "They were going to do the X rays right away, then if it was necessary, they said they'd take him into surgery. The vet said he'd call as soon as he has any news."

"It's going to be expensive, isn't it," Jonathan said. He felt terrible.

"Don't worry about that," said his mom. "Let's just keep up our hopes for poor Winchester." She glanced at Steve. "What's wrong?"

"Wrong? Nothing." But Steve's mouth was set in a grimace of pain.

"Let me see that leg!" Mom cried. She knelt down, raised Steve's leg onto a chair. "Good heavens—your leg is swollen up. Doesn't it hurt?"

"It—yeah. It hurts."

"Probably all that extra weight," said Jake.

"You shouldn't have carried . . . of course, you had to," said Mom quickly. "I can understand it, you had to."

"There's one thing I know," said Steve. "If anything happened to Winchester, and I never even tried to help him, Jonathan would kill me."

"No, I wouldn't," said Jonathan. He gazed at all the food. It looked delicious. But somehow he couldn't eat.

The telephone rang.

Jonathan jumped up to answer it. It was the vet.

"We had to take him to surgery. He's fine now. A little groggy, and, of course, we've got him on transfusions. But I know what caused the trouble. Would you like to see him?"

"See him? You mean—you have visiting hours this late?"

"Not usually," the vet laughed. "But this is an unusual situation. I think you'll agree when you get here."

"Want to stop for ice cream?" Laurel's father asked.

"What about dinner? Won't Mom be mad?"

"Mom's working a little later tonight," he said. "Come on. If you won't tell, neither will I."

They went to the ice cream store. Laurel got a cone with pistachio ice cream on the bottom and almond jamoca fudge on the top.

Her father got the same as always: peach.

"Want to walk a ways?" he asked. "It's a nice night."

"Sure," said Laurel. "I like to walk by the shops when there's nobody around."

"Me too," said her father. He licked his ice cream cone. "I've always adored peach ice cream. Ever since I was a kid. Some things never change."

"I guess I'll be eating pistachio and almond jamoca fudge when I'm an old lady."

He laughed and nodded. "Probably." He kept on walking, kept his eyes on the store windows, never missing a beat. He asked, "Want to tell me what's been troubling you?"

Laurel's heart seemed to skip. She should have known. She felt betrayed—ice cream, a bribe, as if she was a little child. She stopped, thought of tossing the

127

ice cream into a trash bin. No. That would be silly and childish. Besides, she'd rather eat it.

"What's bothering me," Laurel repeated. "Nothing. Why do you ask?"

"Frankly, Laurel," her father began as they crossed the street and continued along the lighted streets, "your mother asked me to talk to you. We are both puzzled. And concerned."

Laurel sighed. She hated conversations that began this way.

"Your math teacher, Mrs. Smith, called your mom at work last week. Did she tell you?"

"Mrs. Smith told me she would call." Laurel shrugged. "She's a jerk."

"What?" Her father's eyebrows flew up in surprise and reproach. "Your teacher?"

"She's always threatening to call people's parents," Laurel said heatedly. "Just because I missed a couple of homework problems."

"Your teacher said you were the best math student in your grade. Everyone had high hopes for you. They are naturally concerned and—ah—disappointed, as I am too."

"I'm sorry." Laurel kept her eyes straight ahead. The ice cream had lost its taste.

"Your mother told her that we are worried too. That since we moved, you have not been the same. You forget your homework. Your flute teacher says you do not practice as before. There too people had high hopes for you, with respect to the Youth Symphony. . . ."

"It's not my fault I split my lip!" Laurel exclaimed.

In her vehemence she struck out; the ice cream fell to the pavement with a plop.

They walked on, faster.

"I chose to play the flute," Laurel said. "Can't I choose not to?"

"If the choice is wisely made," her father replied. "I have the feeling you are choosing out of anger, though. That's not a good way to make a decision."

"Why should everyone have these high hopes for me?" Laurel burst out. "I'm tired of everyone wanting me to do this, do that, be the best, be perfect."

"Nobody said perfect."

"Yes, they did. They do all the time. Perfect! Perfect!" Laurel's voice was low, but her eyes snapped, her cheeks felt flaming. She could not stop now.

"Everything about Mom is perfect," she cried. "Her hands, her clothes, her hair, everything. I'm not like her. I make mistakes. I can't pronounce the Chinese words. The kids laugh at me, call me America Yankee. I lose things. I lost my jade necklace. My grandparents will find out the very first moment. You might as well know it. I dropped the dragon. The golden dragon that Great-grandfather gave me—it is not perfect anymore either. It's cracked."

Her father stopped, took her hands, and looked at her by the street lamp. He smiled slightly, and at last he said gently, "Oh, Laurel. How can I help?"

Suddenly Laurel found herself crying. Tears brimmed over her eyes, slid down her cheeks, blurred the street, the stores, the lights. "You can't help! Nobody can help. I've looked everywhere, I've prayed to find it. I don't take care of things. They get away from me—everything gets away from me. I can't hold onto things."

Laurel's father stared at her, his hands open, a helpless gesture. Then he nodded. "Yes. I see. Without your jade you are unprotected. I'm sorry, Laurel. Truly, I am. I've tried to help you. I even agreed to have Mr. Wu."

"But you don't really believe in him," Laurel said. "You're always worrying about what it will cost. You think it's nonsense."

"How do you know what I think?" Her father looked offended. "I was concerned about the expense. Mr. Wu happens to be a very expensive fêng shui man. His remedies always involve shopping trips. I suspect he gets a commission from every store in Chinatown. But that doesn't mean I think it is nonsense. Laurel, who am I to speak against a wisdom held for thousands of years among my ancestors?"

"Wisdom? Dad, you studied physics and engineering and design. You've told me a thousand times, you studied math. Where are there any spirits in that?"

"What a man studies in books," said her father, "is not the only thing he knows. Look, the fêng shui man speaks of the dragon spirit lying within the hills. His is the breath within the earth, the energy waiting to be used. So Mr. Wu says we must harmonize our buildings with this cosmic breath—how can I say he is wrong? Don't we know that everything in life must be in balance? Maybe there are many kinds of balance and many different names for it."

Laurel felt her face burning. This was a new father. All these years she had seen him only as the architect listening so intently to his clients, concentrating on the precision of his drawings. It always seemed that everything her father did was entirely in his own hands.

"What about—spirits?" Laurel said tentatively. She licked her lips. "Have you ever thought there could be spirits?"

"What sort of spirits?" he asked. He finished his ice cream cone, tossed his napkin into a bin.

"Like—ghosts. Do you believe in such a thing as ghosts?"

"Why not?" He smiled. "Laurel, all these things—spirits, dragons, fêng shui—they are all ways to try to explain the universe. The hidden universe."

"You think there is such a thing?"

"Yes. People have always believed that there are things we cannot see, cannot explain. Whatever these things are—and people call them by different names—the important thing is how we use them. Even Mr. Wu admits that mostly we make our own luck, by how we act and what we wish for."

"How do you know what Mr. Wu believes?" Laurel asked.

Her father chuckled. "Well, he and I have had quite a few talks through the years. I agree with him. When you were very little, that time he first came to the house, Mr. Wu told me you are especially sensitive to . . . to such things."

"He did!" Laurel exclaimed. She smiled in spite of herself—to be special, even in Mr. Wu's eyes, that was really something.

They walked back toward the car. Her father said, "When you were little, you used to sit on the window seat looking out. I used to watch you. Your lips would be moving, but no sound came out. It was as if you were—ah—communicating with someone. Or something. Unseen. And then when you walked away, you always looked kind of—ah—glowing. Happy. So I assume children have this inner life. At least when they are young. Some lose it. Maybe you will lose it too, maybe you never will."

Laurel caught her breath. "What happens to it?" she whispered.

Her father stopped, and by the street lamp she saw his frown. "I don't know, Laurel. Things change. People change. We grow up and stop believing in the same things. That could be bad. Or it could be good."

Laurel felt sleepy and heavy, as if she had been studying for a long, long time, and words were overwhelming. Her father's many meanings seemed to swirl through her mind. He was talking about her childhood. He meant that she was growing up. No longer could she imagine that by wishing she could make things happen her way.

Her father put his arm around Laurel's shoulders and gave her a slight squeeze before he unlocked the car door.

Home again, her father asked Laurel to make some tea. "I'm not hungry for dinner," he said. "Just a cup of tea would do nicely."

Laurel prepared the tea and set it out on the pretty china set. She heaped several fortune cookies into a small glass bowl, then brought the tray to the table and called her father.

He came in, smiling appreciatively. "Ah, very pretty," he said of her preparations.

He opened a fortune cookie, unrolled the paper, and

read: " 'If you want to eat well, compliment the cook.' " He laughed. "Very wise, I must say."

Laurel read her fortune aloud. " 'If you wish to succeed, ask three old people.' " She ate her cookie. "I know only one old person," she said. "Mr. Wu."

"But very soon," said her father, "you'll know two more."

12

*

The vet's office was dark, except for a small porch light, and the vet was waiting for them at the door.

"Come in. Come in. My assistant is with your dog. He's still a bit groggy. The dog, I mean, not the assistant." He laughed.

They went through the dark waiting room and to the operating room with its bright lights and long table and various size cages.

There on a table, lying on his side, was Winchester. A young man wearing an apron leaned over the dog protectively.

Jonathan rushed over to the table and held Winchester's head in his arms. "Winchester, oh, Winchester," he murmured. "You poor dog, I'm so sorry—are you okay?"

The dog opened his eyes, sighed, then closed them again.

"This is what's been giving him all the trouble," said the vet. "It's a miracle this dog is alive. It could have lodged in his windpipe—or anywhere. Actually, I've never heard of a dog swallowing something so large and so elaborate. Of course, cows and horses do it all the time, but dogs . . . it was lodged in the upper intestine."

134

As he spoke the vet reached over onto the counter, scooped up something that glittered, and laid it down on the table.

Mom, Steve, and Jonathan all gasped and talked at once.

"You've got to be kidding!"

"I'll be darned."

"Wow—poor Winchester!"

The vet grinned. "Do you know anyone who has lost a jade necklace?"

There it was, a jade pendant in the shape of a carved circle hanging on a gold chain.

Jonathan's mom looked at him inquiringly. "Do you think . . . ?"

"Laurel," he said. "Boy, I can't wait to tell her."

"What about Winchester?" asked Steve. "When can he come home?"

Winchester groaned.

"Give him a couple more days here," said the vet. "Then you can take him home. If you hadn't brought him in when you did," he said, pointing at Steve, "this dog would be history. Then I noticed you were on crutches. Carrying that dog in here must have set you back some." The vet turned to Jonathan and smiled. "Young man," he said, "your father sure is one heck of a guy."

The words leapt to Jonathan's mouth purely from habit. "He's not my father."

Laurel's dad picked them up from school and drove Jonathan and Laurel to the library.

Jonathan waited until Laurel's dad drove away.

Then he reached into his pocket and said, "I've got something that I think belongs to you."

When she saw the jade necklace, Laurel let out a shriek. "My necklace! Where did you find it?" She did a little dance of joy. "Oh! Oh! I never thought I'd see it again—oh, Jonathan. Thank you, thank you. Where did you find it?"

"Not me," Jonathan said, grinning. "It was inside of Winchester. That's why he's been so listless and sick. The vet had to operate. They saw it on the X ray."

"But how . . ."

"Well, you know how he digs and sniffs down into the ground. I figure he must have found it out in the yard somewhere."

"In the yard," Laurel mused. "I remember I was going to pack it for the move. Then, I remember I put the necklace on and I went to get the wind chimes."

"Maybe it caught on a branch," Jonathan suggested.

"It could be," Laurel said. "I wonder how long it was in Winchester's tummy."

"Probably since the day of the accident," Jonathan said. "Maybe the necklace was caught in the branch that broke."

"That must be what happened," said Laurel. "And then Winchester started rooting around. . . ."

Laurel slipped the necklace over her head. "I'm never going to take it off again," she said. "If I'd been wearing it the day I climbed your tree, I'd probably be in the Youth Symphony today. I might not even have gotten hurt."

"Do you really think so?" Jonathan asked.

"Jade protects a person. If you fall, it takes the fall."

136

"I see," Jonathan said.

"You don't believe me?" Laurel asked.

"I didn't say that." He began walking up the library steps. "It just seems a little farfetched to me," he said.

"Oh. Like a golem? A thing you made out of clay, and it starts attacking your father?"

"He's not my father!" Jonathan shouted.

"Oh. Sorry. I guess I just figured—he does everything for you and he's married to your mom, so I thought . . ."

Suddenly Jonathan felt miserable. He sat down on the low brick wall just outside the library door. "Steve saved Winchester's life," he said. "I didn't even thank him."

Laurel sat down beside him. She leaned her head in her hands.

"I wanted to tell you," she said in a low voice, "none of this was your fault."

"None of what?"

"The bad luck. Things happening to people. I knew about the ghost. Mr. Wu told me I might have to share it. I refused."

"Who's Mr. Wu?"

"The fêng shui man. He said if I couldn't get the ghost to move, I'd just have to share it. I wanted to keep him for myself."

Jonathan looked at Laurel. She looked tired and pale. He took a packet of Starbursts out of his pocket. "Want one?"

She smiled and took the red one. "Thanks."

He asked, "Laurel, do you really believe there is such a thing as ghosts? Or do we sort of—you know—invent them ourselves. Maybe when we have bad vibes—you know—evil thoughts . . ."

"I don't know," Laurel said, chewing her candy. "But even if we invent them ourselves, and if it's part of our evil vibes, then we'd still have to find a way to get rid of them, wouldn't we? I mean, it isn't just enough to say you don't believe in them. Are things still happening at the house? Weird things?"

Jonathan nodded. "My door still rattles in the morning. My mom read this article about poltergeists. Some people back east had stuff thrown through the house all the time by some invisible thing—they finally had to get out and sell the house."

"Whatever it is, and however it got there," Laurel said solemnly, moving toward the library steps, "there must be a way to get rid of it."

"They call it exorcism," said Jonathan.

"Yes. I know."

They went up the steps. Jonathan started to laugh. "I can just see myself going around asking people how to do it."

Laurel laughed too. "Maybe it's in a book in the library."

"Fat chance."

"Maybe," said Laurel, "ghosts are sort of like people. They don't like change. You know?"

"Like you with your grandparents."

"Like you and Steve."

They stood silently for a time. Then Laurel asked softly, "What happened to your real dad?"

"He was killed in a plane crash. I was very little. The thing is," Jonathan frowned, knotted his hands together, "fifty-seven people were saved. Only two died."

Laurel sighed. "Wow. I guess that was sort of a—a miracle."

"Yeah," said Jonathan. "I guess."

Then she turned to glance at Jonathan again. "Maybe the Chinese mirror has helped a little. Nobody's gotten hurt anymore, have they?"

"Well, I can't say things are right at home. Steve had his heart set on that ten-K run. It's next Sunday. He thought he'd be okay by then. And he would have been, if he hadn't picked up Winchester. I found out it's his birthday."

"When?"

"That same day. Sunday. I guess he wanted to get into the race and win—you know, be a hero on his birthday."

"What about Jake?"

"Jake. Well, Jake is staying around for a while."

"That's bad?"

"Good and bad. I love having him around. I just hate his mess. He's so—*big*. He trashes my room. He plays that music all the time. . . ."

"Why is he staying?"

"Freda. He's been seeing her every day. In between they talk on the phone."

"It would be great if he got married," Laurel said.

They both jumped up, grinning, and in accord they rushed into the library to look for Freda.

Freda the librarian sat between Laurel and Jonathan at a large conference table. Books were spread out all over the table, and papers and pens.

"It's interesting," Freda said, "that both of you are actually on the same track."

"How's that?" asked Laurel.

"The dragon represents the unseen power beneath the universe. The golem is also said to represent power, creative energy. . . ."

"You're saying both of them are imaginary," said Laurel.

"Not imaginary," said the librarian, turning to Laurel earnestly. "They are representations of things we feel exist, but which we cannot see. Such things are found in every culture, every religion and nationality, and they go back to ancient times."

"But the dragon is a good spirit," Jonathan objected. "While the golem, it says here," he tapped the book, "is destructive."

"The dragon also destroys sometimes," said Laurel. "In fact, there is a story here about the big dragon killing the little ones, causing disasters like floods and storms that also kill people and wreck houses."

"Both can be destructive," said Freda. "Both can be forces for good. It depends on who uses them. And how."

"Er—excuse me, I wonder if you could help me . . . er, find a list of local real estate agents."

It was Jake. But he looked different. Laurel gave Jonathan a quick wink.

Jake's hair was trimmed. His cheeks were smoothly shaven. He wore a white dress shirt, open at the throat, and neatly pressed blue denims. And his right wrist was no longer bandaged.

Freda turned. "Certainly," she said. Her color deepened. "Jake! Hello. I—ah—your hand."

"I can play my balalaika again," Jake said.

"How wonderful. I've never heard balalaika mu sic."

"So you told me the other day." Jake seemed to bow, and if he had been wearing a hat, you could tell he would be holding it in his hand. "My sister is outside coming to pick up the kids. I thought maybe—we thought—you might like to come over and listen to the balalaika. As a librarian," he said, "you probably need the exposure to such things, especially since you are interested in Eastern European and Russian culture. . . ."

"I'd be delighted," said the librarian. She rushed off, whispered something to the other librarian, and appeared minutes later with her purse and jacket, ready to go.

They persuaded Freda to stay for dinner.

Jonathan had never seen Jake this way—so mellow, so earnest, so tender. Even on crutches, he shot up from his chair to bring Freda a soda, a napkin, another piece of chicken. And it had been years since Jonathan had seen his mother this way—so gentle and relaxed and, well, sort of like the mom he remembered.

She was wearing a long blue skirt and a soft flowered blouse. Her hair was down around her shoulders, held with an ornament of white satin; it shone under the light.

Steve had prepared barbecued chicken and corn bread and coleslaw. Freda praised the food and the fact that Steve had cooked it. "I love to cook," Steve said.

"Oh, your mother trained you well."

141

Steve smiled, shook his head. "I trained myself. Had to. I've been on my own since I was fifteen."

"That's unusual," said Jake.

"Not really," said Steve. "I was raised in an orphanage in Cleveland. One of the last remaining institutions of its kind of the country. I must say, it wasn't bad. Just a little—impersonal. But we learned how to take care of ourselves."

"In more ways than one, I'd guess," said Freda.

"Oh, sure," Steve replied. He put up his fist. "We had to be streetwise."

Jonathan stared. His breath came quick. He seemed to feel things rushing in upon him, sudden realizations—the punching bag, the workouts, the determination to make it, to sell people insurance, so they'd be protected. It all came together.

Jonathan looked at Steve as if for the first time. There were a few gray strands in his dark hair. His eyes were dark too, and very bright, and he didn't talk much. When he did, it was a cheerful kind of talk, patient talk, and some of it wasn't so very interesting. But he seemed to care about people. He wanted them to be protected, maybe because he himself never was.

"Everything is delicious," Freda said with a smile at Steve. "I'm from back east, you know. I've found that lots of people out here don't seem to eat anything but raw fish and stringy things, like sprouts and seaweed. I think it's great to be healthy. But you can take it a little too far."

"I quite agree," said Jonathan's mother with a laugh. "Of course, some people do it only for effect." She glanced at her husband. "They imagine they have

to do whatever is 'in,' or people will think they a.
too old-fashioned."

"Old-fashioned is okay by me," said Freda. She put
out her foot, nodded at her shoe. "Like these shoes.
I've got bum feet, can't walk in high heels. So I wear
these klunkers. You have to know who you are."

"Amen!" said Jake heartily. Then he blushed, patted
his pockets, coughed silently.

"Kids today," continued Freda, "aren't ashamed to
dig back into their roots." She gave Jonathan a smile.
"Like Laurel and Jonathan. They're proud of their
heritages. They don't run away from them, the way
people used to do. Oh, we're a great melting pot, but
that doesn't mean we should all forget our separate
passions, the things we love, the things that make us
different. That's where all the fascination is, and the
zest in life."

"I say, vive la différence!" sang out Jake.

For dessert there was cherry pie. Jonathan's mother
had stopped at the bakery on her way home and
bought a huge cherry pie with streusel on top.

"Remember when we used to have cherry pie back
home?" she asked her brother, looking misty-eyed.
"With streusel?"

"I sure do," Jake said. "Mama made it herself. Oh,
I can still smell that kitchen on Mama's baking
days! You were probably too young to remember,
Marion, but . . ."

"I remember all of it," she said. "Come on. Play us
that ridiculous old balalaika!"

"Someday," Jake said to his sister, "you could do
me a favor."

"Yes?" Jonathan saw his mother dab the corner of her eye with a tissue.

"Get out that old recorder of yours, and play us a tune."

She nodded, and while Jake played, silence was like a curtain hung behind the strumming, lilting sounds. Jonathan saw that every face bore the same look of yearning and sweetness. He wondered whether it showed on his face too.

Laurel's grandparents were coming in just four more days.

Laurel's mother came home with several large packages in her arms and a plastic bag in her hand, in which swam several goldfish, round and round.

Laurel and her father ran out to help. "What's all this?" asked Laurel's dad. "Did you buy out the stores?"

"I went to Chinatown after work. I needed some things, and I know we won't be going on Saturdays anymore." Mom handed him a paper bag. "Here, take this. I've got to get the fish settled properly. Laurel, here, take the goldfish."

Laurel took the plastic bag, surprised by the weight of the water. The fish darted back and forth too swiftly to count, looking like small streaks of gold; then Laurel saw that two were black-and-white spotted, eight were goldfish.

Laurel's dad stood by, shaking his head, frowning. "Jacqueline, you had to go to Chinatown to buy goldfish?"

"No, no, I also bought some more teacups and small plates and two lacquer trays. And a wall hanging. Those walls in my parents' rooms look so bare they will think we are uncultured people here."

In the kitchen her mother prepared the water in the glass bowl, and Laurel put in the long green curls of seaweed and one of the small stone bridges and the colored stones her mother had bought.

When they were finished arranging everything, Mom and Laurel brought the fish tank into the new room, the grandparents' room.

Mom stood back, frowning. "Too small," she said.

"What's too small?" asked Laurel.

"The tank! Too many fish for that small tank."

Laurel stepped back; she knew that tone, and her mom's eyes smoldered.

"That man is a cheat," she cried. "He must have thought me a fool, and I . . . I was too distracted to think, to realize, ten fish! Who would buy so many? Three or six, lucky numbers, sets of two—what a stupid thing to do!" She burst into tears.

"Ma!" Laurel rushed to her mother, sat down beside her on the bed with its brand-new quilt, crisp and ready for the grandmother and grandfather who were coming in just four days.

"Oh, Ma, what's so terrible? We can get a bigger bowl."

But her mother kept her face in her hands, and she swayed to-and-fro, and Laurel heard her muffled whispering, "I can't do anything right. Oh, Laurel, I'm so clumsy. She will think I'm stupid."

Laurel sat back. At last her mother drew her hands away, blew her nose on a tissue. "I'm sorry," her mother whispered.

Laurel reached up and unfastened her jade necklace.

Ma," she said softly, "Jonathan found my necklace. The dog had swallowed it. But don't worry, it's all cleaned up now. I . . . I want you to wear it." Quickly she fastened the chain around her mother's neck. "It will bring you good luck."

Suddenly her mother's arms were fast around Laurel, and the two of them sat close together, hugging.

"My sweet child," her mother murmured. "My sweet child."

"And, Mom, I wanted to tell you. I've decided. I am going back to Chinese school."

"But Laurel . . ."

"I am!" Laurel said. She stood up, pulling herself to full height, as her mom did whenever she reached a decision. "I am *not* going to let those terrible people bully me with their bomb scares. I'm not afraid. Besides, I like to go to Chinatown. It feels . . . very nice."

Her mother stared at her. She said, "I thought the other kids tease you."

Laurel shrugged, hands out. She realized it was a gesture that Jonathan used. "I don't care. Let them tease. What's so terrible? I am an America Yankee—but I'm also Chinese. I belong there as much as they do."

"Listen, Laurel, I have an idea," said Mom, brightening. She was up and bustling, full of energy, picking up the fishbowl. "We will bring some of the goldfish over to your friends. We will divide them in half, five and five. We can stop by the supermarket and get a glass bowl, at least good enough for now. Don't we have more stones and seaweed in the kitchen? Yes, yes, let's go over there right now. Such good friends!

It was so nice of them to return your jade. We mu
repay them with a gift—yes, that is the proper way.

Laurel smiled to herself. If she had heard that word
"proper" once, she'd heard it a million times.

"A small token of our gratitude," said Laurel's mom
soberly as she handed the bowl with its goldfish to
Jonathan's mother. "You were so kind to find Laurel's
necklace."

Jonathan stood beside his mother, beaming. "It was
really Winchester's doing," he said. "I guess if he
hadn't swallowed it, the necklace would still be lost."

"Ah, yes, the dog," said Laurel's mom.

As if on signal, Winchester dragged himself into the
room. He stopped and laid down, his head on Laurel's
foot.

Her mother reached out, protective, then drew back,
smiling.

"Winchester is a good dog," Laurel said hastily to
her mother. "He's my friend." She knelt down and
patted Winchester's head and back.

Later, as they were headed home, her mother said,
"Laurel, I never thought I would live long enough to
see you making friends with a bulldog."

"Life is full of surprises," said Laurel.

13

*

The last four days were like the scene from a speeding car: Everything blurred and flew, and suddenly it was October twenty-fifth, the red-letter day, the circled calendar day. Laurel and her parents drove to the airport hours ahead of time. Nervously they waited and paced, bought peanuts and ate them, bought Cokes and drank them, sat down, stood up, waited and waited and waited.

The plane was nearly two hours late.

Laurel thought she would die of tension.

But when the plane was suddenly announced, and passengers came trotting down the ramp and through the doorway, everything seemed too fast, as if there had been no warning and no time to get settled.

Laurel stood back, searching every face. Men in business suits carrying garment bags and briefcases rushed past. Women in baggy blue pantsuits, their hair knotted oddly, wearing socks and sandals, picked their way into the terminal, looking about for relatives, their faces creasing into smiles or frowns, depending on their expectations.

Laurel felt her heart rise and plunge, rise and plunge. Everything felt strange; her fingertips were cold, her throat dry.

Then she heard the whisper, saw the glint of te
in her mother's eye. "There they are."

What can be said about reunion? Nothing. The
heart knows. There are no words.

Laurel watched as her mother seemed to sink into
the arms of the other woman, and her father and the
older man shook hands, then nodded and reached,
smiled, nodded again. Laurel was lost in the overflow
of their emotion. She felt drained, already invisible,
sinking.

Then clearly, as a bell sounds clear, a voice cut
through the commotion. "Where is Laurel? Your
child? Is this Laurel?"

Hope and joy ran through the question. "Is this
Laurel?" Amazement, as if the questioner beheld
something so precious, so marvelous as to fear the answer. "Is this Laurel?"

"Yes! Oh, yes, Ma, this is my daughter, Laurel!"

It was the sort of embrace Laurel had never felt before, soft and strong and delicate all at once, mingled
with perfume and the rustle of silk.

"Grandmother," Laurel whispered. "Grandfather."
She felt the hard, papery hand in hers, the strong
bones, the pressure of his knuckles, like stones, and
the soft breath from between his lips as Grandfather
kissed her forehead.

They went home. Laurel and Grandmother and
Mother sat in the backseat, the two men in front. Already, their family had changed pattern. Men and
women made one group. The generations made another. The skipping of generations a third. It seemed
as though the future unfurled itself, and Laurel envi-
sioned herself walking between the two old people,

r smiles, her specialness in their eyes. "This is our anddaughter," they would say, a hundred, a thousand mes, with the ring of pride never fading from their voices.

The adults talked. Laurel listened. The flight, the urgency, the endless papers, red tape, the farewells from friends and relations, the house to be sold, possessions packed.

"We had so much that we had to send the gifts," said Grandmother. Her voice was unique. The lilt was Chinese. The words were precise, perfect English. If a painting could speak, Laurel thought, it would sound exactly this way. Grandmother was beautiful, with firm pink lips, large almond-shaped eyes, the smoothest skin Laurel had ever seen on an old person. Her small hands were beautifully, flawlessly manicured, the nails red-tipped and long. She wore a wool suit of pale rose color, and a white blouse, and a gold and pearl pin representing a bursting bouquet of flowers, with gold earrings to match, and her small feet were clad in black patent leather high-heeled shoes. She was altogether beautiful.

And Grandfather, in his tweed jacket, held himself firm and tall, his eyes noticing everything, but silence settling around him, a man who knew it is better to listen than to speak. Yet when he spoke it was in a deep voice, with pauses to let people hear and contemplate. He moved slowly, as if he were aware of the importance of every step and every gesture. And he reached out and placed his hand on Laurel's head, and he said, "We are blessed to have this beautiful grandchild."

With quiet pleasure they looked at all the rooms in

the house. They loved the goldfish swimming in bowl in their room, and Grandmother touched Mon cheek with her delicate finger and sighed, "Ah Daughter, you have thought of everything."

When they came to the parlor, they paused and stood before the portrait of Great-grandfather Lin Peng. Mother took a match and lit the incense stick in its holder. The wick glowed red; the heady smell of incense flowed into the room.

Grandmother and Grandfather, moving as one, stepped back. Gracefully they dropped to their knees, then folded their bodies gently down and touched their foreheads to the floor.

Laurel, watching, saw their movements fluid as a dance, and their expressions serene.

Wordless, Laurel bent her body down to the floor, folded her knees beneath her, and with her mother by her side, touched her forehead to the floor three times, signifying respect and love and the unity of generations.

Then they all went into the breakfast room and sat down to a light meal of tea and soup and fruit and small cakes.

Laurel's grandmother ate the way she spoke, with precision and delicacy, glancing at Laurel every once in a while, smiling, nodding, as if they already shared a secret.

The secret came two days later.

Jonathan was amazed. Hundreds of people had gathered in the parking lot in front of the supermarket at the center of town.

"Hey, Jonathan!" It was Paul Berkowitz from his

.h class, waving, running toward him. "I didn't
.ow you were signed up for the ten-K!"

"Yeah. My—I got signed up a few weeks ago."
Jonathan shifted nervously. "I've never been in a
race."

Bob Warren, a boy from Jonathan's P.E. class, came
up and joined them. "Hi. Isn't this great? There's
about twice as many people out as last year."

"I've never been in a race," Jonathan repeated.

"It doesn't matter how you come in," said Bob.
"All you have to do is finish the race. Some old people enter and come in walking—everybody cheers. It's
really neat."

"Everyone gets a sweatshirt," said Paul, "just for
entering."

He pulled off his windbreaker. Jonathan saw the
logo on his yellow T-shirt, a stylized house printed in
blue, with the Hebrew words *Beit Haim*. Bob Warren
took off his sweatshirt, displaying the same logo.

Before Jonathan could say anything, the coordinator
of the race called through his megaphone, "All right,
everybody, I want you to make five lines over here
and get your numbers. The race starts in twenty minutes."

Everyone hurried and scattered; the crowd con-
verged upon the long table that had been set up for
registration. People rushed about, yelling to their
friends, talking to onlookers, doing last-minute
stretches, fixing their shoes, headbands, sipping water
from plastic bottles.

Beit Haim. Of course Jonathan knew what that
meant. House of Life. It must be the name of the syn-
agogue. And even as he pondered, standing in line to

152

get his registration number, Jonathan saw other yellow T-shirts with the blue logo. They seemed to pop up like wild mushrooms after the rain—kids he knew from school, most about his age, and some older guys and girls, who must be teachers. And then he saw the two of them, Rachel and Rita, dressed alike—Rachel, with that fabulous figure, and Rita, the little redhead, also wearing white running shorts and the yellow T-shirt with the logo *Beit Haim*, House of Life.

Rita saw him and ran over, laughing. "Hi, Jonathan! Isn't this exciting?"

"It sure is," he said. He was laughing too. "Hey, I didn't know you . . . is that the name of the temple?"

"Yes. Our Hebrew class all joined the race together. We had these class shirts made. There are fifteen of us. Eight of us are doing our bar and bat mitzvahs this year."

Jonathan felt as if the wind had been knocked out of him. Rachel and Rita, Paul and Bob—things were taking on a totally different perspective.

"Rachel and I were wondering about you," Rita said. She stretched as she spoke, first one leg, then the other. "We figured you're probably still going to your old shul in San Francisco."

Jonathan shook his head. "No," he said. "I'm about to sign up for—" he glanced at her shirt again. "*Beit Haim*. With the move and everything," he said with a broad smile, "we just haven't gotten around to it yet."

"Oh, great. You'll love it. We have a terrific time. We have parties, and sometimes we go on outings, like to the Tea Garden and the museum. The guys want to start a softball team."

The world seemed to spin suddenly, fed by sparks

gold and silver, like the spinning top Jonathan had when he was very little, and the harder he pushed it, the more the sparks flashed until he was laughing and laughing with joy.

"Everybody! Everybody!" the organizer yelled into his megaphone. "Now, I want everybody over here behind this line. Little kids over on the right—that's it. Lady, please get that stroller out of there. Yes, of course there are prizes for the winner, Larry—we all know you've been training since last year."

Everyone laughed and pushed into places; Jonathan managed to position himself between Rita and Rachel.

When the gun went off, Jonathan bolted forward. But he had begun too fast and realized that he must find his stride. "Take it easy," he murmured to himself. "An even pace. Steady pace. Long strides."

Suddenly, from the sidelines, he heard a squeal. "Jonathan! Jonathan! Go! Go! Go!"

It was his mom, waving her hands and jumping up and down. Beside her stood Steve. He lifted his crutch and with it, waved.

"Where's Jake?" Jonathan wondered.

"Jake! Jake!" he heard his mom scream, and he looked back behind him and thought he'd absolutely crack up, for there was Jake on crutches, joining the race, and Freda walking beside him in bright green shorts and a white tank top, her arms pumping, and she was talking and talking and talking.

Ten kilometers, about six miles, was a distance that seemed at first impossible, then manageable, and finally, too short. Jonathan felt the tremendous pulsing sensations in his legs and chest, the exhilaration of beating out all his angers and all his fears on the pavement. Sweat gathered on his face, sweat soaked roots of his hair and streamed down his sides. lifted his legs higher, pushed out farther, felt talle stronger, even invincible. A chattering commenced in his mind as he pounded faster and faster. "I'm gonna win, gonna win, gonna win this race! I'M GONNA WIN!"

But he didn't win. He didn't even come close to winning. Some guy who had been training for months, a ninth grader, took first place in his category. Jonathan was somewhere in the middle of all the twelve-to fourteen-year-olds, along with Rachel and Rita, Bob and Paul—along with his buddies.

They all gathered at the finish line and drank Gatorade from paper cups. Then they lined up for their sweatshirts, great-looking white shirts with the town logo and the date stenciled in black and red.

"Jonathan! Jonathan!" called his mom, rushing over to him. She was beaming. "Honey, that was great."

"Thanks, Mom. Hey, guys, this is my mom. Mom," he said, "meet Rachel and Rita. They live on our street. And this is Paul and Bob, friends from my school."

"Hello, hello—glad to meet you all." Mom looked so happy. Then Steve came over, held out his hand.

"Congratulations, Jonathan," he said. "Well done. It was a good race."

"Too bad you couldn't . . ," Jonathan began.

"Oh, don't worry," said Steve with a smile. "There's always next year. Besides, I almost had more fun watching you. There's nothing like your first race, is there?"

"Nothing like it," Jonathan agreed.

he woman behind the table leaned toward Jona-
n. "What size?" She had her hand on a stack of
weatshirts, each in its plastic bag. "Medium?"

"No," said Jonathan. "Large."

"But—are you sure? You look like . . ."

"Large," repeated Jonathan. "It's for my dad."

Time took on a different aspect. Where before there
had been this touch of frenzy and haste, somehow,
with Grandmother and Grandfather around, things
moved more slowly and easily. It was like the difference between pumping your bike up a bumpy road or
gliding down a gentle hill.

They talked. Grandmother wanted to hear everything about their lives. She and Mom sat up late into
the night, talking about the days of separation, prais-
ing dear Auntie, long gone now, but still loved for her
generosity and kindness.

"I think I would have been utterly defeated," Laurel
heard Grandmother say, "if I hadn't known you were
safe in America. I couldn't have gone on with you in
danger."

"I missed you," Mom said. She said it often.

"We will make up for lost time," said Grandmother.

Together Grandmother and Laurel sat in Grandmother's room, watching the goldfish play in the
bowl, swimming in and out of the little bridge, hiding
amid the seaweed.

"Pretty, to have fish in the room," Grandmother
said with a smile, "and of course goldfish represent
good luck."

"You believe in luck, Grandma?"

"I certainly do," said Grandma heartily. "How else

156

would we have come to you?" She lowered her v
and spoke behind her hand, her eyes peeping
shining. "Listen, I had a premonition, last year at th
time. I clearly saw the number thirteen, as if it was
written on the air."

"Where, Grandma?" Laurel breathed. She sat on the
wicker hassock, while Grandmother sat on the small
wicker love seat.

"Why, in my own bedroom. I woke up in the night,
and it was as if the numbers were written in the dark-
ness, smoky white letters. Thirteen."

"What did it mean?"

"Why, I can only imagine it meant I would be with
my granddaughter in her thirteenth year, what else?"

"Grandmother," Laurel said tentatively, "do you believe in ghosts?"

"Ghosts." Grandmother pressed her hands together
as if she were praying. She closed her eyes for a moment. When she opened them, they were very bright
and wide.

"This is a big question," Grandmother said in her
dainty, precise English. "I have heard many stories
about ghosts." She laughed, a gentle, high sound.
"Some happened in our own family.

"One time when your second cousin Willard, from
Medford, Oregon, wanted to marry this American hippie, they came to Manila to meet your great aunt, his
mother, who was living there at the time. The girl and
Cousin Willard were at a small hotel. In the middle of
the night the girl had a dream. It was a man, cut in
half, only the top, standing by her bed. And in a loud
voice he called to her. 'GO HOME!' he said. 'We do

157

want you here! We do not want you in our fam-
' ' "

Grandmother looked at Laurel and said softly, "Not
because she was American, but because she was not a
good person, she was very dirty and an irresponsible
person. The next morning the girl and Cousin Willard
went to Great-auntie's house. In the hall, first thing on
the wall, there was a portrait of Great-uncle, who was
dead, and beneath it the shelf with incense and can-
dles. Well, Great-auntie lit the incense to introduce
this new future daughter-in-law and to make the kow-
tow ceremony, like we did here for Great-grandfather
Lin Peng. But as soon as the Great-auntie lit the incense, the girl *screamed*." Grandmother clapped her
hands together, a sharp sound. Then she broke into
laughter. "Well! The girl ran away. The picture on the
wall was the very same face she had seen in the night.
The ghost. You believe this, Laurel?"

Laurel nodded.

"So, there are many, many stories about ghosts, and
many things to know, so we can live with them in
peace. You know some stories about ghosts?"

"Yes," said Laurel. And slowly at first, then rapidly,
with confidence, Laurel told Grandmother the whole
story of Great-grandfather Lin Peng's ghost, and of
Jonathan, her new friend who believed he had created
a golem, and of the mischief this ghost-golem had
done.

Grandmother listened carefully, nodding now and
then, folding her hands close to her face when the
tense moments came.

"Now this ghost is making mischief, you say,"
Grandmother summed up when Laurel was finished.

"It is unruly. Out of control. Well, it has to leave, th.
is all."

Laurel nodded. Then, gazing up into her grandmother's eyes, she asked, "How do you make a ghost
leave?"

Her grandmother looked around, as if to find the
answer in the air, then she gave a slight nod and answered herself, smiling. "You make a big noise."

At that moment Grandfather came in. He carried a
golf bag, which he first put away, then came over to
greet his wife and granddaughter, each with a smile
and a kiss.

Grandmother said, "Laurel wants to know how best
to make a ghost leave a house. What do you think,
Husband? You think a noise?"

Grandfather considered carefully. He sat down on
the wicker love seat, then nodded gravely. "Yes. A big
noise, with Chinese gong and cymbals and drums, and
you scare it away!"

Grandmother stood up, beaming at Laurel. "You
see?"

"Yes," said Laurel, wide-eyed, fascinated. "But
then, what happens to the ghost? Where does he go?"

"Oh, he finds another place, somewhere pleasant
and interesting," Grandmother said. "Maybe here he
would go to the bridge. Ghosts like high places with
a breeze and a mist. And he would not be too far
away from his loved ones. We all would be going
over this bridge for sure every week, once or twice. It
would not surprise me at all," she added with a smile,
"if there were many other ghosts by the bridge. He
would have companions."

Laurel glanced at her grandmother. Was she teasing? But no, her face was serious, her eyes gentle.

"A loud noise," said Laurel. She felt herself starting to smile.

"You know a way to make such a noise to scare away a ghost?"

"I certainly do," said Laurel.

14

*

Jonathan immediately grasped the possibilities. "A big noise? Klezmer music," he said, "with drums."

Laurel grinned. "That's what I was thinking."

"It's not hard to get Jake involved," Jonathan said. "Maybe he'd invite some of the players from his band—Abe Krinski on the clarinet, Izzy Howe with his violin. They could all come to the house and play. I'll play the drum. That makes a big noise, all right. I can add the tambourine for good measure. What a party!"

"What would be the occasion?" Laurel asked.

"A birthday surprise," said Jonathan. They were walking to Laurel's house after school. She had invited him to come and meet her grandparents.

Jonathan had never planned a party before. Certainly, he had never planned a party for his dad.

Dad. The word still sounded strange, almost foreign when he said it. Dad. It sounded okay.

"Who will be invited?" Laurel asked.

"We'll invite you and your parents," Jonathan said. "And your grandparents, of course, if they want to come."

"Oh, I'm sure they would love to come. They want to learn about American ways. My grandmother said

ndfather has been reading about baseball. And they
ought me a present. Something that every American
hild has, they said. They saw it in the movies, they
said."

"What is it?" Jonathan asked.

"It's a surprise," said Laurel. "They said it is coming any day."

"So we'll have your family, and Jake, of course,
and Freda, Abe and Izzy with their instruments. What
about food?"

"I can bring Chinese fortune cookies," said Laurel.
"My mother makes wonderful Chinese dim sum."

"My mom can fix her famous tofu burgers," said
Jonathan with a laugh, "and Jake will send out for deli
food—what a banquet!"

"I'll bake Steve a cake," Laurel said.

By the time they got to Laurel's house, it was all
planned.

Laurel's grandmother met them at the door. Her
eyes were very bright, and she was smiling. "Laurel!
I am happy to see you. And you brought your friend.
Jonathan?"

Jonathan and Laurel's grandmother shook hands.
"Would you like some refreshments? Come in. We
have ice cream. We went to the store today. Pistachio," she said, "and almond jamoca fudge. Very
American flavors." She laughed.

They ate the ice cream and sesame cookies. Laurel's grandmother had cookies and tea.

"Where is Grandfather?" asked Laurel. "I wanted
him and Jonathan to meet. Jonathan is a baseball
player. He also has a baseball card collection, don't
you, Jonathan?"

Jonathan nodded. "Maybe your husband would ... to see them," he said politely.

"I'm sure he would, but he and Laurel's father have gone to the airport to pick up . . ." She paused, smiling, and she put her hands over her mouth. "The surprise for Laurel. It arrived."

"Why wouldn't they deliver it to the house?" asked Laurel.

"When it comes," said her grandmother, "you will see why."

The automobile horn sounded. A few minutes later Laurel's father and grandfather came in carrying a crate between them.

"You must be Jonathan," said the grandfather. His eyes twinkled. "I hear you are a great runner and a good friend to our granddaughter."

"Thank you, sir," said Jonathan, shaking hands. Then he did something he had never done before. He ducked his head and made a short bow.

"Come and see what we brought," said Grandfather.

Laurel had already run over to the crate, and she stood before it, her hands clasped under her chin. Jonathan had never seen her look so excited. She stood there speechless, her breath coming in short gasps.

"What is it?" Jonathan asked

"Oh, Jonathan, it's the most adorable little . . ."

"Sharpei," put in the grandfather. "Chinese dog. We heard in America every child has a dog, and they treat it like a baby! They put it on a cushion and feed it tender morsels. Well, we wanted our granddaughter to have everything she needs."

Laurel's father opened the crate with a screwdriver. He reached in and brought out the little dog. It was

163

and silky; its brow was deeply furrowed, and the ṣall eyes peered out anxiously.

"Laurel loves dogs," said her father with a wink at Jonathan. "Don't you, Laurel?" he laughed. "In fact, one of her best friends is a bulldog."

Laurel made a cradle of her arms and cuddled the puppy inside. "Oh, Little Dragon," she sighed. "That's going to be your name. You look just like a friendly little dragon."

"A perfect name," said Laurel's grandmother, clapping her hands.

"He will guard the house," said her grandfather.

"Maybe he'd like to meet Winchester," said Jonathan.

"Except for one thing," said Laurel's dad. "He is a girl."

"Dragon girl," said Jonathan with a grin. He reached out, and Laurel placed the puppy in his arms.

Jonathan kissed the soft head, felt the pulsing little heart, looked at the face still groggy from the long trip. He held the pup close, then handed her back to Laurel.

"Bring Dragon Girl to the party on Sunday. Winchester needs a friend."

The party! All week long the telephone rang. Jonathan called with new ideas, plans, reports.

"Steve doesn't know a thing. Mom thinks it's a fantastic idea. We're storing all the food at Rita's house. So of course we've invited her and Rachel to come. Mom said I should invite a couple of the guys, so I did. Jake said to be sure and bring your flute."

"Why?" Laurel had trouble getting a word in.

"He wants you to play with them."

"But I don't know the music," Laurel objected.

"Sure you do. Jake says you're a natural."

"What? How would he know?"

"He says he could see it in your face the last time you were here. Bring your flute."

So on Sunday, along with her mother's dim sum and a chocolate cake with vanilla icing and pink hearts, and Little Dragon on a new leash, Laurel and her entire family arrived at Jonathan's house.

"This used to be our house," Mom was explaining. "We sold it and got the larger house because you were coming."

Grandmother nodded. "My first American party," she said. She looked so pleased that she seemed ready to cry.

"Listen," said Grandfather. "American music."

From the porch they already could hear the sounds. Boom! Boom! Boom! Adum-dum-deedle-doo.

Laurel laughed. "Well, I suppose it is as American as anything else."

Jonathan and his mother and several friends brought them inside, exclaiming, murmuring, "Come in! Come in! We're so happy to see you. What an adorable puppy! Winchester! There's someone we'd like you to meet."

All the usual commotion reigned—laughter, talk, the rattle of dishes, the enjoyment of food, the discovery of things in common, friendships begun.

For Laurel all that faded into the background, as she swiftly put together her flute. She stood for a moment just listening. Jake sat on the sofa, strumming his guitar. Behind him stood the fiddler, gently strok-

his strings, and on the other side famous Abe
ᴋrinski, sweating profusely as he blew note after in-
ᴘired note out of his clarinet. Never had Laurel heard
such a sound.

Laurel picked up her flute, held it to her lips.

Jake gave her a nod.

Abe Krinski winked.

The fiddler smiled.

And Laurel played. She played long, singing notes
to flow in between the beep beep beeble of the clarinet. She played scales running up, then down, to min-
gle with the soft violin and guitar strummings, and
then she played billows of sound, improvisations,
tunes that leapt out and meandered back again, tunes
that inscribed circles of harmony and sent out streams
of notes to challenge the others. Oh, they met her
challenge, they joined her theme and went even further, then came together again, the pace quickening,
the notes squealing and reaching and tumbling.

Out of the corner of her eye Laurel saw Jonathan
take up the tambourine, and it added a cascade of
sound. She saw Steve reach for the big drum, and he
sat on the low stool beating it. Boom! Boom! Solemn
and deliberate, until in a burst of pleasure he let the
beat take him away.

On and on and on they played, song after song,
until at last, exhausted and exhilarated, the musicians
stopped for breath, and there came a patter of ap-
plause.

"Laurel, that was great!" cried Rita and Rachel.

"You guys should play for bar mitzvahs," said Bob
Warren.

"And weddings," said Laurel's mother.

"Speaking of weddings," said Jake. He wiped his brow, patted his pockets, reached out for Freda's hand. "Freda and I have an announcement to make. Not to detract from this wonderful occasion of my brother-in-law's birthday party, I will only say that you may expect to hear some good news shortly."

There was general laughter, a gasp from Jonathan's mom, tears, then Jake added in a loud voice, "And you will all be invited!"

Laurel's grandmother disappeared with Jonathan's mom into the kitchen. They came out carrying a cake on a tray, singing,

> *"Happy birthday to you,*
> *Happy birthday, dear Steve . . ."*

The klezmer band took up the tune, first Abe Krinski on the clarinet, then the fiddle, then the flute . . . and to everybody's surprise, a new instrument joined in. Jonathan's mother on the recorder. Like a voice, only better, the recorder sang it.

> *"Happy birthday to you,*
> *Happy birthday, dear Steve . . ."*

The others joined in again. They played it straight. And then they bent it and squeezed it, they lengthened it, blasted it, accelerated it, wound it down to the same simple melody, "Happy birthday to you!"

The musicians put their instruments away in that certain slow silence that follows a frenzy. Jake wiped his brow.

"The girl is good," said Abe Krinski.

"Good? She's terrific," said Izzy Howe.

"Well, I guess we've found ourselves another member of the klezmer band," he said to Laurel. "If you are willing, that is."

"I'm willing," said Laurel. "When's our next gig?"

"Wait for the announcement," said Jake with a grin. "Soon."

"Talented child," said Laurel's grandmother. "I hear you will soon play in the Youth Symphony too."

"It runs in the family," said Grandfather proudly. "My second cousin once removed on my mother's side played the flute."

While everyone packed up and said their goodbyes, Laurel and Jonathan went out to the side yard, where Winchester and Little Dragon waited together.

Winchester lay on his side. Little Dragon danced around him, nipping playfully at his ears. The bulldog rolled his eyes and pulled back his lip in what seemed like a foolish grin.

"Look, he loves it," said Jonathan.

Laurel sat down on the grass. Jonathan joined her. She asked Jonathan, "When Jake and Freda get married, will they live with you guys?"

"No," said Jonathan. "Jake wants to get an apartment in Sausalito. I'll be able to ride my bike down there."

"What about your mom's job?" Laurel asked.

"It's over," said Jonathan. "But my mom isn't too worried. She says that now she has other options. She wants to take her time and think about it a while."

Laurel's pup ran into her arms. She cuddled her Little Dragon close.

Jonathan glanced about. He whispered, "Do you think it worked? The loud noise?"

Laurel listened. No shadows. No sounds. Only the gentle late afternoon breeze.

"I think it's gone," she whispered. "What do you think?"

Jonathan nodded.

Laurel asked, "What about that golem of yours?"

"Well, according to tradition," said Jonathan, "one rubs out the golem by erasing the letter *aleph* inscribed on his forehead. The remaining letters spell death and the golem simply crumbles, like dust."

"Is that what you did?" Laurel asked. She wasn't sure whether or not he was serious.

Jonathan laughed. "Not exactly. Yesterday afternoon Winchester came into my room. He noticed the fish tank on my table. Apparently he was fascinated and wanted to get a closer look. Somehow he got hold of my model."

Jonathan held out his hands in a gesture of finality.

"You could say that Mogul the Muscle Man, alias golem, is now pulverized, thanks to Winchester."

Laurel laughed. "Thanks, Winchester!"

Jonathan and Laurel whistled. Both dogs, huge Winchester and small, dainty Little Dragon came running.

And they all went in together to join their families.